Bolan started to squeeze the trigger

Suddenly the security guard stepped directly behind his target. The Executioner let up, fearing his penetrating 9 mm rounds would drill through the terrorist and into the old man. But his caution proved futile. Even as he relaxed his trigger finger, the al Qaeda killer twisted at the waist and sent a burst of fire from his Uzi into the uniform.

The old man fell to the ground.

Bolan's jaw tightened as he redirected his aim at the man with the Uzi. But the terrorists had disappeared through the door into the Bass Pro Shop.

The Executioner reached the top of the steps and jumped over the body of the security guard. There was nothing he could do for the old man now.

Except kill the men who had taken this innocent life, and no doubt many others.

That was exactly what he intended to do.

D0696401

MACK BOLAN ®
The Executioner

The Executioner®

Don Pendleton's

SOFT TARGET

A GOLD EAGLE BOOK FROM
WORLDWIDE®

TORONTO • NEW YORK • LONDON
AMSTERDAM • PARIS • SYDNEY • HAMBURG
STOCKHOLM • ATHENS • TOKYO • MILAN
MADRID • WARSAW • BUDAPEST • AUCKLAND

First edition October 2005
ISBN 0-373-64323-3

Special thanks and acknowledgment to
Jerry VanCook for his contribution to this work.

SOFT TARGET

Printed in U.S.A.

He who knows when he can fight and when he cannot will be victorious.
>   —Sun Tzu, c.400-320 B.C.
>   *The Art of War*

I will bide my time and I will find a way to defeat the murderous plots of evil men. I will not allow the slaughter of innocents.
>   —Mack Bolan

Prologue

Hal Brognola heard the door open behind him as he slipped the videotape from the plastic cover. He turned to see a big man enter the War Room, letting the door swing shut behind him. Brognola and Mack Bolan had been friends for years. Both knew how grim the current situation was, and there was no time wasted exchanging pleasantries. A simple nod of the head was their only greeting.

Brognola turned back to the video player beneath the big flat-screened television set on the stand against the wall. He jammed the tape into the slot, then took a seat to Bolan's left, halfway down the table. With the remote control, he turned on the TV first, then hit the Play button.

The screen turned a dark fuzzy gray. A few seconds later, a man wearing black BDUs and a wraparound face mask and headdress appeared. Brognola hit the Pause button to give Bolan a better look. A Russian Tokarev pistol hung from the web belt around the man's waist. On his left hip, opposite the Tokarev, a curved, broad-bladed *jambiya* had been thrust under the belt. The eyes above the mask were little more than slits—what Bolan assumed to be the inevitable result of long years in the desert. The skin around the slits looked coarse, wrinkled, as dried out as a slab of beef jerky.

"Any ID on him?" he asked.

Brognola shook his head. "Nothing positive. CIA thinks he may be one of several Taliban men who went merc after Afghanistan and contracts to various terror organizations." He brought a fist to his mouth, coughed into it, then went on. "He'll be speaking Arabic. The translation is at the bottom of the screen." He hit the Pause button again, and the picture started to move.

The camera moved in for a close-up as the man began to speak in a passionate voice, spouting a long tirade of anti-West propaganda. Bolan studied the eyes above the face wrap more closely. Almost hidden within the slits, the tiny black orbs were not the wild, crazed eyes of a fanatic. They looked cold, calculating, purposeful.

They looked like the eyes of a deadly snake.

As the masked man preached, the camera panned back to reveal that he was in the desert. The subtitles disclosed that his words were an ardent call for all Muslims to watch the tape, use it in their own training and then attack Americans, Israelis, or other infidels who might stand in the way of setting up a worldwide Islamic theocracy. Those who died in the process would be rewarded in Paradise.

The camera angle shifted slightly to the right, and suddenly what appeared to be an American shopping mall filled the screen. It looked out of place amid the desert sand surrounding it. Signs announcing stores like JC Penney, Dillard's, Elder-Beerman, and others could be seen, and automobiles of all shapes and sizes filled the parking lot.

The camera zoomed in closer and men, women and children—all wearing jeans, shorts, T-shirts, and other western dress—could be seen entering and leaving the many exits.

It had taken Brognola three viewings of the footage before he noticed several dozen men, some alone, some in pairs, approaching the mall entrances. They blended in almost perfectly—all walking nonchalantly toward the different entrances wearing the same type of clothing as the other mall patrons. What set them apart was, while many of the shoppers carried large shopping bags as they left the mall, these men carried large bags in their arms as they *entered*.

Mack Bolan caught the subtle distinction immediately. From the corner of his eye, Brognola saw Bolan's eyes narrow. The Executioner's jaw tightened slightly.

The screen went black for a moment, then another camera came on inside the mall. Across the wide hallway, Brognola saw the tobacco shop and shoe store he had seen so many times already. Typical sounds of mall chatter, plodding footsteps and an occasional shout or laugh could be heard.

A moment later, six of the men who had infiltrated the mall suddenly jerked Uzis and MP-5 submachine guns from their bags. Bursts of automatic fire exploded above the other sounds as they aimed the weapons at the high ceiling above them. As the bullets drilled holes, the chatter and laughter of the shoppers turned to shrieks of terror. Four of the gunmen left the camera's range, but it was evident they were entering various stores in that wing of the mall. The two who remained in view quickly gathered the people in the hallway into a crowd and forced them to their knees, hands clasped behind their heads. One elderly man who held a cane pointed to his knees and shook his head.

The effort earned him a quick burst of 9 mm autofire in the chest as his white-haired wife covered her mouth in horror.

The camera zoomed in on the face of the man doing the shooting. They were the same eyes Brognola and Bolan had seen just a moment before, and the face still wore the wrap-around mask.

The camera panned back and forth across the hallway to show more screaming women, crying children and terrified men being driven out of stores into the common area. When all six terrorists had returned, the man in the face mask gave a nod. One of the other men—mockingly clad in a red, white and blue T-shirt which read *USA* across the front—shouted in heavily accented English. The shoppers rose to their feet.

Another elderly gentleman, who had been able to lower himself but could not get back to his feet, was also shot by the man in the mask. A young woman screamed over the roar of the gunfire. She leaned over the man and received her own burst of fire.

The terrorist leader fired randomly into the crowd. Three more hostages—one woman and two men—fell to the ground. Then the camera zoomed in, and the masked man's lips began to move again. The subtitle read simply *I told you to be quiet.*

The men with the submachine guns herded the survivors down the hallway to the tables in the center of the food court where they were forced into seats. The man in the mask assigned one team of terrorists to stand back and cover the frightened captives. Other teams began taking individual hostages out of their chairs and off to the side where, one by one, they were searched. The camera followed and showed one of the searchers finding a small snub-nosed .38 and a badge in the purse of a middle-aged woman. He held the trophies up to the camera with a wicked smile, then pressed the police woman's own gun against her temple and fired.

A young man was carrying a lock-blade folding knife. The same grinning terrorist used it to cut his throat. More gunfire sounded whenever anyone, male or female, resisted the search in any way. Several of the shoppers were shot for what appeared to be no more than a scowl on their faces.

Brognola glanced at the big man at the end of the conference table. The Executioner's jaw had now tightened so hard Brognola thought it could snap.

The man in the mask pulled a cell phone from his pocket and tapped in three digits. It was obvious the numbers he dialed were 911. A few moments later, his lips moved and the subtitles at the bottom of the screen revealed that he was demanding television, radio and newspaper coverage. He also agreed to speak to a police negotiator.

Brognola broke the silence. "There's about five minutes here now of nothing but intimidation," he said, and thumbed the Fast Forward button of the remote. The images on screen danced by at superspeed, then the masked man reached into his pocket for the cell phone again, and Brognola slowed the video once more.

The big Fed and Bolan watched negotiations between police and the terrorist leader go back and forth. In between calls, several news cameras were allowed in. The masked man shouted accusations of Western imperialism, greed, false religion and even Satanism, while terrified reporters and cameramen shot footage of the hostages before being chased out at gunpoint.

Suddenly, one of the terrorists appeared on the screen holding a suitcase. He opened the case to reveal a complex series of wires, tubes and other equipment. No one viewing the tape could have mistaken it for anything other than what it was—a bomb.

Without warning, all of the terrorists turned their guns on the people still seated at the tables and began firing. Gunfire drowned out the screams as people fell to the tiles or slumped over tables. The massacre went on for what seemed like hours. But it was all over within thirty seconds—Brognola had timed it with his wristwatch.

When the last body had fallen, a clean-shaven terrorist who looked no older than twenty drew a pistol. He walked through the rivers of blood, administering a final head shot to any of the hostages still breathing. The masked leader walked toward the camera, said a few final words, then stepped back. From another pocket he produced a remote-control device similar to the one Brognola held in his hand. With the same dispassionate expression he had displayed all along, he pushed a series of buttons.

An ear-shattering explosion could be heard from the audio portion of the tape. The screen went black.

Brognola hit the Pause button. "All simulated, of course," he said, turning to face Bolan. "An al Qaeda training film. One of our Special Forces teams came across it when they were cleaning out the caves in Afghanistan. There's more, if you want to see it. One similar strike at a large Christian church—Sunday morning service. Another that looks like the courthouse of some small Midwestern county. Then there's a—"

Bolan shook his head. "I've seen all I need to see," he said.

"Their strategy is simple. Infiltrate, take over suddenly and violently, and immediately kill anyone who even looks like they might not behave like a sheep on its way to the slaughterhouse."

Brognola nodded in agreement. "The only reason they negotiate is to get face time with the media. The demands they make are only stall techniques. They don't expect them to be met." He paused, cleared his throat and then added, "In fact, they don't want them to be met."

Bolan nodded. "They know from the beginning that they're going to kill the hostages," he said. "And they know they're going to die, too. They blow themselves up and wait for the rewards their leaders promised them."

"That's about the size of it." Brognola stood. "But there's more you should know. Aaron and his team have been picking up all kinds of stepped-up chatter on the Internet. It seems al Qaeda's about to start a whole new wave of strikes, and it sounds like they're leading up to something big. *Very* big."

The Executioner didn't respond. He just stood and started toward the door.

Brognola looked at the broad muscular back threatening to burst the tight blacksuit at its seams. If anyone could take down the man in the mask before innocent people started getting killed, it was Mack Bolan. "So what are you planning to do?" he asked.

The Executioner opened the door and turned back to face his old friend. "I'm going to do whatever it takes to stop those terrorists."

1

The clothing on the Executioner's back was as foreign to his nature as feathers on a German Shepherd dog.

Bolan left the pro shop in a red, three-button short-sleeved polo shirt, brown slacks and white golf shoes. On his head he wore a baseball cap embroidered with the words *Oak Haven Country Club* and the club's logo—a sturdy, towering oak. Around his waist was a thin leather belt with a small silver buckle, and across his broad shoulders was the strap to a plaid golf bag. Various woods, irons and a putter extended from the open top of the bag.

Unless you counted the golf clubs as potential bludgeons, he appeared unarmed.

Bolan made his way down the paved footpath toward a stand of trees on the west side of the fourteenth hole. The trees lay roughly halfway between the tee where Congressman Milo Alley would set up after he'd played the first thirteen holes, and the green he'd be aiming toward.

Another grove of trees stood directly across the fairway from where Bolan planned to set up. A third cluster of elms stood seventy-five yards farther south. It was Bolan's hope that he could cover all possible sniper blinds from his central location.

As the Executioner neared the trees he reached down, unzipping the side compartment to the golf bag. Two balls and half a dozen loose tees dropped to the asphalt as he took another step, then turned and dropped to a squat to retrieve them. Stuffing them back into the bag, he closed the zipper again, stood and continued on.

The dropped balls and tees had allowed him to do a fast, and final, 360-degree sweep of the golf course. He'd seen several men and women on the surrounding fairways. More on the greens. None of them had paid him any attention. No one looked like he or she was planning anything except the next shot.

Bolan ducked into the elms. As soon as he was hidden within the thick branches and leaves, the Executioner leaned his golf bag against the trunk of a tree, then unzipped another outside compartment and produced a small cellular phone. The remote earpiece was already plugged in, and he stuffed the plastic hearing device in his left ear, then tapped in a series of numbers.

A moment later, the familiar voice of his old friend and fellow soldier Jack Grimaldi came over the air waves. "Howdy, Sarge," the pilot said. "What's your handicap today?"

The Executioner heard the whine of the surveillance helicopter in the background. He and Grimaldi had fought more wars together than he could count, and there was no one he trusted, or respected, more than Stony Man Farm's top flyboy. "Working with an old worn-out pilot's my main handicap," he said. Then turning serious, he said, "You have visual on Alley, Jack?"

"Not at the moment," Grimaldi replied. "I'm doing my best

to stay high enough not to be noticed. But I'm watching the screen, and the homing device you planted in his golf bag tells me he's on the ninth green at the moment."

"Okay," Bolan said. "I'm setting up. Let's leave the line open."

"You got it," Grimaldi said. "About the time he hits the thirteenth tee I'll drop down a little lower."

The Executioner clipped the phone to his belt, then pulled all of the clubs out of his golf bag and let them fall to the ground. Reaching into the bag, he felt the axis of a folding rifle stock brush his fingers. He pulled the long gun out, unfolded it, then leaned it against the tree next to the bag.

Digging deeper into the bag, the Executioner found the shoulder rig with the Beretta 93-R. It had been custom designed to hold the machine pistol with a long tubular sound suppressor attached. Bolan shrugged it over his arms and across his back. Near the bottom of the golf bag, his fingers felt the grips of the Desert Eagle, and its nylon inside-the-waistband holster. He stuffed it into his slacks on his right side. A razor-edged combat knife was removed and clipped at the small of his back. Last, from the very bottom of the golf bag, the Executioner lifted a wadded nylon windbreaker. It was far too warm for a jacket of any kind, and wearing one would draw attention. But if, for some reason, he was forced away from the cover of the elm trees, it would cause less concern than wearing his pistols openly.

The Executioner lifted the rifle and checked to make sure the scope had not been jarred out of place. Pulling the bolt up, back, then forward and down again, he watched the gleaming brass of a 30-06 hollowpoint round disappear into the chamber. Bolan had sighted a weapon at 300 yards just that morning. If his shot turned out to be considerably longer, he would have to adjust for bullet drop. Shorter than 300 yards, and it would be necessary to shoot low.

Moving to the edge of the trees facing the fairway, Bolan dropped to his knees and began gathering clumps of leaves and broken twigs. When he had built a small hill-like firing platform, he returned to the golf bag and opened yet another side compartment. A moment later, he was nestling into the mound with the barrel of the rifle resting on a sandbag. He looked through the scope, moving right and left across the fairway toward the grove of trees on the other side. He had a clear shot no matter where the man preparing to kill Congressman Alley decided to set up.

Bolan drew in a deep breath, let it out, then relaxed, letting his mind replay the chain of events that had brought him to the Oak Haven country club golf course in the Washington, D.C., suburb of Georgetown.

Leo Turrin, one of Stony Man Farm's best undercover operatives—had been developing informants within the ranks of al Qaeda and other Islamic extremist groups for several years. Even before viewing the training tape, Bolan and Brognola had seen intelligence reports that shopping malls, Christian churches, Jewish temples and other public sites were potential targets for terrorist strikes. One of Turrin's informants had also put them on to the fact that single assassinations of politicians, and other public figures, were planned on the street, in their homes and on golf courses.

In the past, all of the informants' intel had been general. But this time, Turrin had received a call that a *specific* hit was in the works.

The Executioner's eyes scanned the trees again but he saw no sign of life. He glanced up and down the fairway. Even with the details Turrin's man had given them, Bolan knew there were still a thousand variables that could not be determined until the last second. And any of those variables, misread or miscalculated, could make his counterattack go wrong. He would have to think on his feet and adapt accordingly, and quickly, to whatever happened in the next half hour or so.

Speaking quietly into the hands-free mouthpiece, the Executioner said, "Jack, you still with me?"

"Of course," Grimaldi's voice came back.

"Where's Alley now?"

"He and his party are just behind the sand trap on twelve."

Bolan frowned. "Then our man ought to be showing himself pretty soon."

"Yeah, but there's no sign of him from here," Grimaldi said. "And I went ahead and risked a couple of lower sweeps."

Bolan nodded. The sweeps might have seemed low to Grimaldi but they were still high enough that the Executioner had missed them. Stony Man Farm's number-one pilot was good at his job. "Okay," he said. "Stay loose and keep me informed."

The Executioner turned his face to the right, frowning toward the third grove of elms he knew lay beyond the thick branches and leaves in front of him. On the same side of the fairway as he'd set up, he considered this third cluster the least likely choice for the al Qaeda assassin. The grove was not nearly very large, and the asphalt footpath leading from hole to hole did not come as close to it as to the other two. Anyone who entered it would have to leave the path and walk nearly fifty yards across open ground—toward an area that had nothing to do with golf. Such action might not be like whirling red lights and a siren going off, but it could draw unwanted attention just the same.

The Executioner turned his attention back to the elms across the fairway. He still saw no sign of anyone inside. Whispering, he said, "Jack, as long as you're risking a little low flying, see if you can see anything in the trees just south of me."

"Just did," Grimaldi replied. "All clear." The pilot paused. "Forget it, Sarge. You're still the best sniper around, and if your instincts tell you you'd pick the grove across from you that's where any other pro would go."

"I was just thinking along the same lines," Bolan said. "But there's one problem with that logic, Jack."

"Okay. I'll bite. What?"

"Who's to say this al Qaeda man thinks like a pro? There's no guarantee he's not just another form of 'suicide bomber' they sent out half-trained." He paused a moment to let it sink in, then went on. "If that's the case, there's no guarantee he'll know enough about what he's doing to find the best place to set up." He paused again. "My instincts are *my instincts,* Jack. Not necessarily *his.*"

"Point taken," Grimaldi said.

"So where's Alley now?"

"Just sank his putt on the twelfth. Looked like he bogied to me."

The Execution settled back into position, reminding himself that he had no choice but to play the odds. As he'd told Grimaldi, any sniper worth his salt would choose the grove of trees to the east of the fairway as his hide. It offered the best field of view as well as the clearest path of escape after the shoot. But if the sniper was, indeed, an amateur as Bolan feared he might be, all bets were off.

"They're teeing off on the thirteenth right now," Grimaldi said suddenly in Bolan's ear.

"How many in the congressman's party?" the Executioner asked.

"Four," Grimaldi said. "Two men, two women. The other man is Hiram Hennessy. Multimillionaire entrepreneur and big contributor to the congressman's campaigns."

"They playing with their wives?" Bolan asked.

"Don't know, Sarge. But I wouldn't count on it."

"How's that?"

"Well, the women look to be thirty to forty years younger than the men. Both of them blondes." The pilot chuckled softly. "They look like they just stepped off the runway to me." Grimaldi laughed again. "My guess is they still have their g-strings and pasties on under their golf togs. Besides, there's way too much pinching and giggling going on for anybody to be married."

"Okay," the Executioner said. "Hold tight. Let me know if you see anything around the south grove. And tell me when they get to the fourteenth tee."

"Roger."

Bolan closed his eyes for a moment, resting them. There was a strain to combat, but it was nothing like the strain of waiting. And watching. The eyes got weary quickly, and when the assassin was finally spotted and the game began, he might have to go without blinking for minutes at a time as he tried to line up a shot. He turned to the south once more. Something was bothering him about those trees—something he couldn't quite figure out.

Nodding, the Executioner turned back again. In a microsecond, he made the decision to alter his plan of attack. If the would-be assassin hadn't shown up in the trees across from him by the time Milo Alley and the rest of his party teed off for the fourteenth hole, he'd grab the rifle and begin making his way toward the grove of elms farther south.

The seconds ticking away felt like hours as the Executioner continued to wait, watching the elms across the fairway. The only movement he saw was a few sparrows that suddenly took off for parts unknown as a squirrel scampered up a tree after them.

"Damn!" Jack Grimaldi suddenly said in the Executioner's ear.

Bolan stiffened. "What, Jack?"

"Sarge, I think we've made a mistake."

The Executioner sprang to his feet, the rifle in his fist, and took off, making his way through the thick trees toward the open area that separated him from the grove of elms to the south. "What is it?"

"Our boy isn't setting up where we thought he would," Grimaldi said. "But he isn't in the trees to the south, either."

The Executioner froze in his tracks. "Where is he?"

"On top of the pro shop," Grimaldi said. "Assembling the parts of a rifle he just pulled out of an old guitar case."

Bolan stood where he was for a brief second, running a mental image of the immediate area through his mind. He remembered the short wall running around the flat roof of the rectangular pro shop. It would provide more than adequate cover for the al assassin from anyone shooting at him from the ground. Bolan had to get to the pro shop, then find a way to the roof. And he had to it fast—before Milo Alley and his party finished driving their way down the dogleg into the sniper's field of vision.

The Executioner hesitated a moment longer, knowing that a second spent planning would save many seconds later, when it mattered most. The fastest route to the pro shop would be to sprint to the fairway, then angle past the fourteenth green and take a direct path toward the front of the building. But from his vantage point on the second story the sniper was bound to see him, and could zero in on him as if he were a duck in a shooting gallery. Bolan would be dead in his tracks, and if he died, so would Milo Alley.

Turning suddenly, he sprinted back through the trees to the path running behind the grove, then cut to his left, the needle-like cleats of his golf shoes sinking slightly into the warm asphalt as he ran. If he stayed behind the trees, they would still serve as cover. But he would have an open and unobstructed run as he circled toward the man on the roof.

With the rifle in his right hand, Bolan grabbed the cell phone in his left and held the instrument to his head. He whispered, "Where do we stand, Jack?" His knees continued to rise and fall as he raced on.

"Alley and the rest are about halfway down the dogleg," Grimaldi came back. "And our buddy on the roof is tightening his scope."

The Executioner came to the end of the first grove of elms He ground to a halt just before the clearing. "Is he looking my way?" he asked the chopper pilot.

"I can't tell," Grimaldi said. "He's facing your way. But I think he's preoccupied with the scope." He paused. "Want me to just land on the roof and—"

"Negative," Bolan said forcefully. Grimaldi couldn't land the chopper, a rental, and shoot at the same time. All he was likely to accomplish was getting himself killed. With Dragon Slayer on the other side of the world with Charlie Mott, the chopper had been hurriedly rented as soon as they'd learned what was about to go down. It was not equipped with bullet-resistant glass or any of the other protective features found on Grimaldi's usual ride.

"You landing is a final option," the Executioner said. "Stay in the air unless there's no way I'm going to make it in time."

With another deep breath, the Executioner sprinted from behind the trees and into the open. He kept his eyes glued to the roof of the pro shop, perhaps two hundred yards in the distance. He saw what he thought might be the top of a head slightly above the wall.

Within seconds he was behind the second grove of elms to the south.

Bolan continued to run, following the pathway as he made the long, looping semicircle that would leave him sixty to seventy-five feet from the pro shop. In the distance to his right, he saw several golfers stop walking and stare curiously across the space that separated them. Golf was not a fast game, and anyone sprinting at full speed was an oddity. The Executioner wondered if they would make out the rifle in his hands at that distance. He doubted it. But even if they could, all they'd do is call the police, and it would be several minutes before officers responded.

What was going to happen concerning the sniper, Milo Alley, and the Executioner—good or bad—was going to go down in an instant. The police couldn't assist Bolan in his efforts.

Nor could they get in his way.

"Bring me up-to-date, Jack," the Executioner said between breaths as he bolted on. He was approaching the end of the second grove of trees. The back edge of the pro shop, including the short retaining wall around the top, was visible. But Bolan could see nothing of the sniper. The man would be closer to the front, still hidden by the trees.

"The guy up top is locked and loaded," Grimaldi reported. "He's propped the end of the rifle barrel over the wall, but he's not even holding it yet. Right now, he's just hunkered down and watching the green."

"Alley and the others?"

"Just the other side of the trap from the green," the pilot said.

"Stay up high unless he looks like he's ready to shoot," Bolan replied.

As he neared the end of the elm grove, Bolan saw the sniper in is mind, making his last-minute preparations. The question was, *when* would he take his shot. The Executioner knew if he was on the roof, he'd wait until Milo Alley was on the fourteenth green, standing over his ball, ready to putt. No matter where the ball might be on the carefully manicured grass, the shooter would have a clear shot at either the congressman's temple, or between the eyes to the brain stem. And he could be certain the man wasn't going to move until he swung his putter. There would be several seconds to line up the crosshairs, take a deep breath, let out half of it and squeeze the trigger.

But, the Executioner reminded himself, that's what a professional would do. Giving the man on the roof too much credit for being professional was what had led to this mad, last-second dash, in the first place.

The al Qaeda hit man had not picked the best spot to set up. There was no guarantee he'd choose the best time to shoot, either. But to kill the congressman it only had to be good enough.

Running on, the Executioner wondered how the sniper had reached the roof. If he'd used a ladder, it had to be on the far side of the building; Bolan had just passed all the other walls of the pro shop and hadn't seen one. Or, there could be a staircase inside the shop that led to the roof.

Bolan had to figure out how to get to the roof. If he entered the pro shop, even if there was such a staircase, he'd waste valuable seconds looking for it. And if he circled the building, he might not find a ladder there, either. As he neared the end of the trees, Grimaldi's voice came over the phone again.

"They're on the green," the pilot said. "One of the women is putting. Alley is still walking toward his ball. Man on the roof is in the prone position now. Pressing the stock into his shoulder. Wiggling around, trying to get comfortable. You know that drill better than I do."

The Executioner realized what he had to do. And, as had happened to him so many times in the past, the plan occurred to him and was formed in a millisecond.

If the sniper had waited this long, he wouldn't fire until Milo Alley stopped at his golf ball—even the rankest of amateurs knew there was no sense shooting at a moving target when a stationary one was about to present itself.

Whether he would wait for the congressman's turn to putt or not was a toss-up. But in either case, Bolan knew he had only seconds.

Breaking out of the trees, the Executioner shoved the cell phone back onto his belt, dropped his rifle and sprinted toward the side wall of the pro shop. Measuring his steps, he left the ground on his left foot, stretching upward like a basketball player about to slam dunk the ball. At the very top of his leap, his fingertips grasped the top of the retaining wall, and he felt the rough concrete tear at his skin. For a second, he hung there against the side of the wall, the weight of his body pulling down against his fingers. He pulled himself up, the muscles in his hands, arms and back screaming protest against the effort. With both arms straining, he was forced to leave the Desert Eagle and Beretta in their holsters.

The thud of two-hundred-plus pounds slamming into the wall of the pro shop had reverberated through the small building and alerted the sniper. As Bolan's head came up over the side of the wall, he heard an explosion. A wall of compressed air seemed to press against the left side of his face, and he knew the sniper's bullet could not have missed him by more than an inch. As he was dropping his head below the retaining wall, the Executioner glimpsed the man behind the rifle working the bolt to chamber another round.

Like Bolan himself, the al Qaeda assassin wore a golf shirt and slacks. Black curly hair extended from the sides of his white baseball cap.

Bolan knew he had one chance. Pulling his right hand away from the wall, he swung down and to his left, clutching the top of the wall one-handed. Another explosion boomed over his head, and he felt the impact as the bullet hit the wall next to his hand.

The sniper was shooting at his fingers.

Jerking the Desert Eagle from its holster, Bolan let his body swing farther to the left, then strained to lift himself as he swung back to his right. The hand gripping the big .44 Magnum revolver made it halfway up the wall, then he fell back to swing away again. Riding the sway as far as he could, the Executioner attempted to build up enough force in the opposite direction to get his face and gun back over the top. This time, he fell just inches short.

Another rifle round exploded on the rooftop and another high-caliber bullet just missed the Executioner's fingers. With the muscles in his left arm threatening to cramp, Bolan threw himself to his left this time as he fell away from the wall once more. Then, with another Herculean burst of strength, he pulled up as he swung back again.

A third round from the sniper's rifle struck the retaining wall, and the Executioner's hand began to burn. He could not be sure if the round had actually struck his fingers or hit close enough to scorch them. But even if he'd been hit, he had retained enough grip to hang on, and as concrete shrapnel and dust blew up into the air before raining over his head, he rose high enough to hook right his elbow over the wall and aim the Desert Eagle at the sniper.

The sniper's eyes widened in surprise. His mouth fell open in awe.

Bolan pulled the trigger. The bullet struck the man under the chin, blowing away half of his throat and severing his jugular.

The sniper was dead before he hit the tar covering the roof.

Bolan pulled himself onto the roof, rising to his feet just as Grimaldi set the chopper down at the other end of the building. He walked quickly to the bloody body on the roof, holstered the Desert Eagle and looked out over the golf course.

All movement on the fairways and greens had stopped as golfers stared toward the clubhouse.

Dropping to one knee, the Executioner patted down the dead man and found no other weapons but the rifle. The man's pockets were empty but around his waist Bolan found a cloth money belt. He jerked hard on the front of the belt, and the Velcro in the back tore loose. The Executioner heard the crackling of folded papers. Hidden in the thin nylon, he could feel several objects in addition to the paper. But there was no time to do a further examination.

In the distance, Bolan heard the sirens as police cars converged on the golf course. He thought of the rifle he had abandoned below, and decided to leave it for the police to dispose of it.

Opening the passenger's door to the helicopter, the Executioner slid up onto the seat.

"Sorry to disobey a direct order and land." Grimaldi smiled as Bolan buckled himself in.

"I'll forgive you this time," the Executioner said.

Without another word, Jack Grimaldi took them skyward.

"Back to the airport?" Grimaldi asked as he continued to pull back the control stick.

"Yeah, Jack," the Executioner said. He turned his attention to the money belt in his lap. Inside, the Executioner found a neat stack of fifty-dollar bills in front of another packet of hundreds. He set them on his lap and pulled out six extra .270-caliber hollowpoint rounds, which he assumed were for the sniper's rifle—he had not had time to check the caliber of the weapon. He tossed them back into the belt and zipped it shut.

In the lower of the two pockets Bolan found a .32 ACP Kel-Tec pistol and an extra magazine for the tiny polymer weapon. To the side were a set of car keys and a motel room key card. At the very back of the pocket, folded lengthwise into quarters, were several pages of computer paper. Unfolding them, the Executioner saw they were typed in Arabic.

Without a word, Bolan handed them to Grimaldi who glanced down, then stuffed them into his brown leather bomber jacket. He would take them back to Stony Man Farm for translation.

As the chopper began to descend near the small private rental agency where they'd picked it up, the Executioner looked down at the key card. On one side was an arrow showing which way the card should be inserted into the door. On the other he saw a sunset and the words, Sun View Motel.

Bolan unclipped the cell phone from his belt and tapped in a number that would eventually reach Stony Man Farm. The call would automatically be rerouted through several countries before it reached the Farm. For anyone interested, tracing it to the counterterrorist facility hidden in the mountains less than a hundred miles away would be all but impossible. The conversation would also be scrambled.

Barbara Price, Stony Man Farm's mission controller, answered on the first ring. "Hello, Striker."

Bolan pictured the honey-blonde seated at the control desk. The only thing that could outshine Price's beauty was her professionalism. "Barb," the Executioner said. "I need a fix on the Sun View Motel."

"D.C.?" Price asked.

"D.C. area, at least," the Executioner said.

"Stand by."

After a short pause, Bolan heard Price say, "Striker?"

"Yeah, Barb," he answered. "What've you got?"

"Only Sun View Motel I'm showing in the area is across the Potomac in Virginia. South of Alexandria, near Fredericksburg, just off I-95."

"I'm heading that way," he informed her.

"I'll tell Hal," she said.

THE EXECUTIONER guided the Buick Century Custom past Francis Scott Key Park and the Star Spangled Banner Monument, then drove onto the Key Bridge linking Georgetown to Virginia. As the waters of the Potomac glistened in the fading sunlight below the bridge, he glanced down at the dashboard. The Century wasn't the fastest car around, but it did have some power. And it perfectly fulfilled a more important need Bolan had at the moment—it's neutral silver-tan color and inconspicuous lines faded perfectly into the sea of other automobiles surrounding him.

Dusk had fallen over the interstate and surrounding area by the time the Buick's headlights picked up the road sign announcing the Rappahannock River in five miles. As Bolan neared Fredericksburg occasional houses and small businesses began to appear. He took an off-ramp just before the river. As soon as he reached the frontage road paralleling the interstate, he saw the large sign in his headlights. Unlike the picture on the key card, the motel sign itself featured a bright blazing sun that would have looked more at home in Florida than northern Virginia.

Twisting the steering wheel, the Executioner turned the Buick into the parking lot and circled the building. The Sun View was a two-story, second-rate lodging with no more than forty to fifty rooms. A small swimming pool—the water a stagnant green and begging for a health inspector—had been sunk in the middle of the horseshoe-shaped structure. Several automobiles sat in the parking spaces outside rooms but, all in all, it didn't look as if the motel was doing much business.

Bolan drove to the front of the building, stopping the Buick at a spot where he could see into the lobby. He had the key card, but he had no idea which of the rooms it opened. He saw a dark-skinned man with straight black hair rise from behind the counter where he had obviously been looking for something. The man leaned forward and rested both elbows on the countertop in boredom.

Bolan drove the Buick around the corner to the first empty parking space, killed the engine and got out. He glanced at himself quickly in the side mirror. He looked too hard in his leather jacket. He needed to look the part for what he was about to do. Walking to the trunk, he popped the lid, opened his suitcase and pulled out a green cardigan sweater. After a quick glance around the parking lot to make sure he'd drawn no curious eyes, he quickly removed the black leather jacket and covered his weapons with the cardigan.

From a small bag next to the suitcase, the Executioner produced a pint bottle of gin. Taking a quick swig, he rolled the liquor around his mouth, then spit it out. Tipping the bottle into the palm of his left hand, he applied more of the strong-smelling gin to his face and neck like a high-school boy who'd just discovered cologne.

Recapping the pint bottle, the Executioner held it in his left fist as he closed the trunk. He checked his reflection in the mirror again. He still wasn't going to pass for some harmless tourist. But at least he looked a little less aggressive in the sweater, and with the odor of gin encompassing him like an alcoholic cloud, bottle in hand, and a little luck, he hoped he could pass for an inebriated traveler who'd accidentally stuck his key card in the wrong door.

The Executioner started at room number 101. Dropping the plastic card into the lock, he watched the light on the electronic mechanism. The bulb remained red. Moving to the next doorway, he did the same with the same result.

At room 106 he had just turned to move on when the door swung open and a rotund man in a ribbed white undershirt stepped out onto the walkway. Thick black hair shot up out of the scoop neck of the shirt both in front and in back, and his arms looked equally simian. "What the fuck you doing, man?" he demanded

Bolan could smell the man even above the gin on his own face and neck. The Executioner knew he was not the only man at the Sun View Motel who'd hit a bottle that night.

Flashing his friendliest drunken smile, Bolan said, "Sorry buddy, wrong room." He held up the gin bottle, shrugged in embarrassment, then turned his back to the man. As he walked on he heard the door slam shut again.

As soon as it did, the Executioner retraced his path back to room 107. The light stayed red when he inserted the card, as it did on the rest of the rooms on the first floor. Climbing the set of metal steps that led to the rooms above, Bolan applied more gin to his neck as he walked to room 201 at the far end of the walkway. Again, he began making his way along the doors across from the iron railing that encircled the building.

When he reached room 215 the light stayed red, but he heard the doorknob turn. His right hand was ready to grab the Beretta under his sweater when the door swung open.

A woman with long brown hair stood smiling in the doorway, a red rose tucked behind her right ear. Other than the rose, she wore only red high-heeled pumps.

She had obviously been waiting for someone. But that someone wasn't the Executioner, and the smile on her face was suddenly replaced with a look of shock and horror.

The Executioner slurred out a drunken-sounding "Sorry, wrong room," then turned and walked on as another door slammed behind him.

Bolan moved on, trying each door he came to, making as little noise as possible. Behind the closed curtains the lights were on in some rooms, off in others. When he came to number 229, directly across from the same steel stairs that had brought him to the second story, he noted the illumination through the window behind the shades.

The Executioner dropped the Sun View Motel key card in the slot. After so many wrong rooms, he was almost surprised when the light flashed green and a click sounded in the lock. Setting the gin bottle quietly on the brick frame beneath the window beside the door, he drew the Beretta from under his arm and reached for the knob.

2

The Executioner had learned over the years that sometimes the best action was inaction. He decided it was best to do nothing. At least for a while.

Bolan stepped to the side of the door as two more explosions sounded inside the room, and another pair of splintery holes appeared in the pressed wood. With his back against the brick between the door and the window, he held the Beretta down at a forty-five-degree angle and waited. No more shots were fired, and as the roar died down he heard excited chatter coming from the room.

He recognized the speakers were using a dialect of Arabic.

Ten seconds went by as the voices argued among themselves. Then twenty. Several doors along the second floor opened and heads shot out like curious turtles coming out of their shells. But when the Executioner turned to face them, gun in hand, they disappeared even faster and the doors slammed again.

Bolan waited. By now someone who'd heard the gunfire would have called the police. But he still had several minutes before they'd arrive. While the fake Justice Department credentials he carried—compliments of Hal Brognola—would probably pass the scrutiny of the local cops, he couldn't afford to get tied up in bureaucracy. He needed to be finished at the Sun View and gone by the time the boys in blue arrived.

Another minute went by with no change in the situation. The men behind the door continued to argue. He couldn't understand, but the Executioner could guess what the quarrel centered around.

There was no back way out of the rooms—he had seen that plainly when he'd circled the premises in the Buick. All they could do now was stay where they were—knowing the same police Bolan wanted to avoid would arrive sooner or later and take them into custody—or rush the door, and take their chances with whoever it was outside on the second floor concrete walkway.

Sirens sounded far in the distance. Bolan knew if the cops arrived and took the men in the room into custody, he'd lose all chance of getting any intelligence out of them.

Yes, he thought, sometimes inaction was the best action. But even then, eventually, somebody had to make the first move.

Bolan shifted the Beretta to his left hand, drew the Desert Eagle with his right, then exchanged hands once more. With the thunderous .44 Magnum revolver, he aimed at the top of the window, well above the head of anyone who might be standing inside the room. For all he knew there might be hostages inside with the terrorists.

The Executioner squeezed the trigger three quick times. The Desert Eagle roared, drilling holes through the glass and cracking the pane all the way down to the brick frame. As the third massive hollowpoint round broke the glass, Bolan stepped away from the window to the door of the motel room just to the left.

Just as he'd expected, the door to room 229 suddenly swung open and a tall man gripping an Uzi in his fists screamed as he leaped out onto the walkway.

Bolan had already set the Beretta's selector to 3-round burst, and now a trio of 115-grain hollowpoint rounds burped quietly through the sound suppressor and into the terrorist. The white T-shirt he wore over his faded blue jeans turned instantly crimson. The al Qaeda man jerked forward, flipped over the rail and turned a somersault in midair before landing on the hood of a parked car. .

A second man had started out the door behind him. But when he saw what was happening, he threw himself back inside. Bolan swung the Desert Eagle toward him a second too late, and there was no sense wasting a round on the door frame.

Bolan stared past the broken window to the gaping doorway. Trying to enter it would be like turning himself into a framed picture with bull's eyes painted on his head and chest. On the other hand, the time for inaction was over.

The sirens in the distance were drawing nearer with every second.

The Executioner took a deep breath and stepped out to the rail in front of the window to room 229. It was time to do the unexpected. Taking two quick steps, he crossed his arms over his face and throat, left his feet and hurled himself through the already cracked glass.

Landing on his side just inside the room between the wall and a table, the Executioner took in the scene quickly. The television was on, tuned to the FOX News Network, and while the story of what had happened earlier at the golf course was not playing, Bolan new that it would have.

Suitcases and other bags were open on the bed, clothing and other items crammed haphazardly inside. The men had been hurriedly packing to leave. Five minutes later, and Bolan knew he'd have missed them altogether.

The Executioner scrambled to his knees, the Desert Eagle still in his left hand, the Beretta in his right. For the two men who remained in the room had had ample time to arm themselves since the first shots had been fired. Now, one held another Uzi while the third cradled a 12-gauge pump-action shotgun.

Both guns were aimed at the doorway.

Seeing a man suddenly crash through the window was something the terrorists had not expected, and while their heads swiveled toward the Executioner—their mouths dropping open in shock—they were a second slow in swinging their weapons his way. And a second's head start was far more than he had ever needed.

The Executioner trained the big .44 on a man of medium height but powerful build, the Beretta on a short and wiry figure wearing a Florida Marlins baseball cap. But Bolan's heart sank slightly as he pulled both triggers, knowing there was no way to take either man alive for questioning.

A pair of .44 Magnum rounds took the stocky man in the upper part of the chest and the neck. The shotgun tumbled to the cheap yellowish carpet, and the terrorist fell on top of it. As his lifeblood pumped from his throat, the yellow carpet began turning a sickly orange.

At the same time, a 3-shot burst from the sound-suppressed Beretta drilled through the wiry man's chin, nose, and left eye, practically beheading him. He froze in place for a second, looking like something out of a cheap, straight-to-video horror movie, with both hands still gripping the Uzi. Then he, too, tumbled forward.

The sirens in the distance were close, and Bolan knew he was almost out of time. Grabbing the Uzi and shotgun off the floor, he tossed them onto the bed and quickly searched the fallen bodies. Both men's pockets were empty but, like the sniper, they each wore money belts. Stuffing the belts into the pockets of his cardigan, Bolan felt the tail of the sweater swinging back and forth under the weight as he hurried to the suitcases.

Other than the weapons, the bags contained only clothing and toiletry items.

As the screaming sirens grew ever louder, the Executioner dropped to his knees and pulled the bedspread up over the mattress. Under the bed, he found a black leather attaché case. Jerking it out, he tried to flip the catches, but they were locked.

For all the Executioner knew it might contain plans for a dozen new terrorist strikes. But he didn't have time to open it.

Holstering both pistols, the Executioner grabbed the case and hurried out the door. He took the steps two at a time, stopping at the bottom only long enough to rip a third money belt from the chest of the man who had gone over the rail. Then he cut across the pool area toward the Buick. Red and blue lights were flashing through the entryway ahead of him, and he could hear excited voices through the open windows of the patrol cars.

There was no way he'd get back to the Buick without being spotted. He'd have to hope that with his cardigan sweater, attaché case and gin aftershave he'd look benign enough that the cops would ignore him.

Bolan glanced down at the pockets of his sweater, bulging and drooping with the three money belts. They were bound to draw attention. Setting the case down next to the pool, he wrapped all three belts around his waist, secured them with the Velcro fasteners, then buttoned the cardigan to his throat. The sweater not only concealed his weapons and the belts, it added a good fifteen pounds to his frame and made him look even more out of shape and, therefore, harmless.

The Executioner affected a slight limp as he emerged from the courtyard into the parking lot. Black-and-white patrol cars were at every corner of the lot, with men in blue racing toward the building while others stood guard at the cars, radio mikes in one hand, pistols in the other.

The Buick was only a few feet away. Bolan started toward it.

He had gone less than ten feet when a voice behind him yelled, "Freeze!"

The Executioner kept walking.

"Freeze or I'll shoot!" the voice shouted.

Bolan had reached the Buick and turned to step down onto the parking lot from the sidewalk. He pretended to see the uniformed officer holding the Glock in both hands in his peripheral vision, and jerked his head in surprise.

"Freeze!" the patrol officer yelled once more. "This is your last warning!"

Bolan stood where he was, the shocked look still on his face.

"Drop the case, turn around and put your hands in the air!" the man in blue ordered.

The Executioner's surprised face turned to one of confusion, as if he didn't understand the man's words. He raised his right hand and began finger-spelling in sign language. He had no idea what he might be saying. But the cop didn't seem to, either. And Bolan saw the man physically relax as he realized why the man he had shouted at hadn't complied with his orders.

The officer motioned for Bolan to set down the attaché case, and the Executioner complied. As soon as he'd straightened again, he lifted his hands slightly over his head like a man who had watched enough cop movies to know what came next. "I am sorry," he said. "I cannot hear."

The lights, sirens, running men and other pandemonium continued all around them as the officer nodded his understanding. A quick expression of sympathy covered his face. He took his left hand off the gun and twirled his index finger in a circle, indicating that the Executioner should turn around. Bolan nodded, then did a 180 as the cop walked up behind him.

The police officer was still going to check him out. But at least he had dropped his guard.

Bolan heard the officer's gun slide back into its holster and a second later felt hands on both shoulders as the man started to pat him down. It was the moment the Executioner had been waiting for—by the placement of the hands, he knew the exact position of the head.

The Executioner hated to do it. The officer was just doing his job, and had exhibited compassion when he realized the man he held at gunpoint was deaf. But Bolan saw no way around it.

Whirling back around, the Executioner drove an elbow into the man's midsection. The strike bent him over in spite of the thick Kevlar vest beneath his uniform blouse, and a rush of air escaped his lips. The Executioner lifted him back to an upright position with a short left uppercut, then drove a right cross into the cop's chin.

The police officer fell to the pavement like a sack of cement.

Bolan glanced around, saw that no one had noticed the quick one-sided fight and bent over the unconscious man at his feet. Dragging him safely out of the path of the Buick, he laid him out on the sidewalk and returned to the car.

A moment later, he had backed the Century out of the parking space and was turning out of the Sun View Motel's parking lot.

THE EXECUTIONER TOOK I-95 across the river and into Fredericksburg, pulling off onto an access road on the outskirts of the city. Driving along the road until he came to an all-night supermarket, he turned in and parked the Buick beneath an overhead light in the parking lot.

Bolan set the money belts on the seat next to him. All three were identical to the one the sniper at the golf course had worn, and he suspected he'd find similar items inside.

All three belts contained more fifty- and hundred-dollar bills, another trio of the tiny Kel-Tec pistols and folded pages of computer printouts—in Arabic.

Bolan dropped the money belts back on the seat next to him. He stared at them for a moment, then unclipped the cell phone from his belt with his left hand. Maybe he had found something useful and maybe he hadn't. The translations would tell. But, in the meantime, there was no use letting any grass grow under his feet.

Resting his forearm on the steering wheel, Bolan looked down at the lighted digits of the cell phone glowing in the semidarkness. He was about to tap in the number to Stony Man Farm when the instrument began vibrating in his hand. Pressing the button he answered the call.

"Location?" Barbara Price asked.

"I'm in the parking lot of a supermarket in Fredericksburg," he said.

"Okay," Price said. "We've translated the papers you found."

"Great. I've got more coming at you ASAP." Bolan paused and let out his breath. "What do they say?"

"First," she said, "we've got a positive ID on your sniper. Bear hacked into the Georgetown morgue's computer files and downloaded a set of fingerprints the medical examiner rolled when he got the body."

Bolan smiled. Aaron "The Bear" Kurtzman was Stony Man Farm's resident computer genius. The program he couldn't crack with enough time had yet to be invented. "So?"

"His name's Hammid Jabar," Price said. "Saudi national. And definitely al Qaeda."

"Surprise, surprise," he said. "Go on."

"Most of the paperwork you found on him was your typical we-hate-the-west-and-let's-kill-the-great-Satan propaganda."

"I'm hoping the first word of your next sentence is 'but,'" Bolan said as Price stopped for breath.

"Then you'll be a happy man," the mission controller replied "*But* two of the pages are outlines for two more snipings."

The Executioner tensed. "Where and when?"

"One of the times has already come and gone without incident. A New York State senator was giving a speech in Central Park at 0800 this evening. He did. But nothing happened."

"That's probably because the shooter died earlier today," Bolan said.

"That's Hal's opinion, too. On the other hand, al Qaeda may have encountered some other technical problems and canceled the hit. Happens sometimes. To the bad guys as well as the good."

"Too bad it doesn't happen to the bad guys all the time," the Executioner said. "Tell me about the third sniping."

"It's set for Springfield, Missouri. Tomorrow morning."

"That's a long way from New York," Bolan said. "Which means they probably didn't have Jabar set up as the shooter, and it's probably still on." Silently, he estimated the flying time from New York to Missouri. "It would be possible for a man to shoot the senator in Central Park and still get to Springfield for the job in the morning. But it would cut things pretty close. Besides, it wasn't as if al Qaeda had a shortage of manpower. Especially if they were using snipers no better trained than Jabar had been."

"Hal said the same thing, in almost the same words." She paused a moment, then went on. "I swear, sometimes I think you two are just two bodies hooked into one central brain somewhere."

"We are," Bolan said. "The brain is Bear's Computer Room. Where's Jack?"

"The closest place he could land was the Fredericksburg police airport," Price said. "Knowing you'd be headed for Missouri, he traded the chopper for one of the Lears." She paused again, and Bolan could visualize her looking at the wall clock and calculating the speed and mileage in her head. When she spoke again, she said, "He should have touched down just a few minutes ago."

"Great," the Executioner said. "So how do I get there?"

Price gave him the directions.

"Thanks, Barb," Bolan said and ended the call.

Getting out of the Buick, the Executioner walked to the back of the car, retrieved his leather jacket and tossed the cardigan into the trunk. He shrugged into the jacket as he slid behind the steering wheel again, then pulled out of the supermarket parking lot.

Missouri, he thought as he and headed toward the Fredericksburg police airport. The Show Me State.

3

Carl Jennings tapped the pen against his temple as he looked down at the weekly time sheet on top of his desk. Where had he been last Thursday at 1330 hours? What had he been doing? Probably filling out one of the other countless, senseless, repetitive, redundant, bureaucratic forms that took up most of his time. The fact was, he spent about ten percent of his time actually working for Homeland Security. The other ninety percent was taken up documenting that work and justifying his—and the administration's—existence.

Jennings knew he was a paper pusher. There was no getting around it. He had become what he had always sworn he would never be, what he had always hated. He was a bureaucrat surrounded by other bureaucrats, generating ream after ream of paperwork that had little, if any, meaning, and there was no way he could kid himself into thinking he was anything more.

Jennings leaned away from the desk in his swivel chair and stared at the time sheet from a distance. It didn't look any better. What was its purpose? he wondered. On the surface, it was to show how he'd spent his week. But Jennings suspected that the real reason for the weekly reports was less honorable. The

HS brass had to know that no one could ever fit everything they did during the week into those neat little boxes where you entered assigned codes.

So, Jennings suspected, the main reason for this minute-by-minute chronicle was to force people to guess at things. In other words, make them lie.

Then, if the supervisors didn't like you, they could always pull out the time sheets and with a little investigative work, prove that your weren't where you said your were, doing what you said you were doing, at the time you said you were doing it. And suddenly, you're fired.

Jennings tried to make himself return to the time sheet but couldn't muster the willpower. He walked to the door of his office and closed it. If he was going to sit idly at his desk daydreaming again, it wouldn't do to let one of the other agents pass by and see him. Like all bureaucracies, this one had its share of snitches who were always looking for ways to sacrifice their peers in order to further their own careers.

As he walked back toward his desk, Jennings caught a glimpse of a group portrait on the wall and stopped. He turned to the picture. Before him, he saw a younger version of himself. He was surrounded by the rest of the members of his fraternity at Yale, and they were all dressed in their blue-crested blazers. The four-story, 150-year-old frat house could be seen behind them.

Jennings shook his head. He thought how naive he had been in those days. He had actually bought into the lie that hard work would get you what you wanted. He had worked his ass off getting simultaneous undergraduate degrees in

prelaw and accounting. He had then gone on to Yale's law
school where he'd learned to work even harder.

Jennings laughed. What he had wanted back then seemed
so childish now that he'd been out in the real world a while.
He had wanted to be a spy. He had wanted to serve his country, to travel the world saving Americans from enemy nations
and terrorist attacks. Of course he'd wanted to sleep with
beautiful, mysterious women in the process. Maybe play a little baccarat and roulette at the casinos in Monte Carlo, as well.

What Carl Jennings had wanted, and had actually thought
possible in those days, was to be James Bond.

Feeling the blood rush to his face, Jennings turned away
from the picture and returned to his chair. The closest he had
gotten to anything exciting was still so far away from adven-
ture it made him want to scream. When he wasn't justifying
his time by filling out the weekly activity reports, he was
evaluating the security around nuclear missile installations.
And that wasn't even done on-site. He sat at his desk and
pulled diagrams of the sites onto his computer screen, then
went down a list of three-hundred-odd questions, answering
each one with a number using a numeric scale. When he finished each report he handed it over to a computer nerd who
ran it through his own programs to check further for weaknesses. In other words, they didn't even trust him to know
what was safe and what wasn't.

Jennings swiveled suddenly to face the wall and the rest
of the pictures that hung there. During his final year of law
school, Jennings had applied to the CIA, NSA and the FBI—
if nothing else came through he'd hoped he could at least work
counterintelligence at home. But then, just a few months be-

fore graduation, September 11, 2001, had occurred and the whole world had changed—especially the intelligence bureaus.

Suddenly, America had a brand-new agency called the Department of Homeland Security, and Jennings had been one of the first to apply. In a rush to get set up and running, DHS had immediately arranged for a background investigation, polygraph exam and interview. By the time he got his law degree he already had the job.

A knock at the door tore Jennings from his reverie, and he turned around in his chair. "Come in," he said wearily.

He felt even more weary when the door opened and the portly figure of Keith Bradley, dressed in his usual short-sleeved white shirt and solid black tie, walked in. The man from accounting held a manila file in one hand. In the other was another of the seemingly endless printed forms that DHS had come up with.

"We've got a problem," Bradley said as he took a chair directly in front of Jennings's desk and set both the file and form on the desk.

"I'm sure it's earth-shaking, whatever it is," Jennings said.

Bradley didn't respond to the sarcasm, but Jennings hadn't expected him to. The fact was, he suspected the chubby bureaucrat had taken the remark at face value. Bradley was the kind of man who believed that minor accounting glitches were capable of starting World War III.

Bradley nodded gravely. "Your receipts don't match up to your expense declaration," he whispered conspiratorially.

Jennings extended both wrists. "Put the cuffs on," he said with the same blank expression.

"No, no," Bradley said, shaking his head back and forth.

"It's not that kind of mistake at all—it's actually in your favor." He leaned forward and opened the file to reveal a stack of receipts. "Which doesn't, of course, make it any less serious."

Jennings forced a concerned frown and mimicked Bradley's nod. "Certainly not," he said but once again his irony was lost on the accountant. As Bradley began sifting through the receipts, Jennings glanced down at his gold Seiko wristwatch—1645. Fifteen minutes and he could cross another worthless day off his calendar. Finally, he said, "Well, how much is it? The mistake, I mean."

"A dollar seventy-eight," Bradley said. He shook his head as if something tragic had happened. "I've gone over it three times now, and I can't find it." He turned both the file and expense sheet around to face Jennings. "I need you to look them over."

"Tell you what," Jennings said. "You just keep the money and we'll both quit worrying about it."

A look of horror fell over the sagging jowls on the other side of the desk. "Oh, we can't do that," Bradley said, shaking his head back and forth.

"Why not?" Jennings asked. "It's less than two dollars."

Bradley's pudgy face changed from horrified to puzzled, and Jennings could readily see that the word "why" was simply not in the man's vocabulary. Men like Bradley did things the way they did them because they'd been told to and, as far as they were concerned, that reason was good enough.

"Why?" Jennings asked again, suddenly taking a sadistic pleasure in pushing the issue. "Why can't we just forget it?"

"Well . . ." Bradley stammered. "They won't let us."

"They who?" Jennings asked.

Bradley looked more confused than ever.

The enjoyment Jennings was deriving from baiting the man died almost as quickly as it had come over him. Sighing, he rose from his chair and walked to the coat rack in the corner of his office. "It's too late in the day to worry about it right now, Keith," he said. "Tell you what. Leave the file here, and I'll look at it in the morning." He pulled his trench coat off the rack and threw it over his arm.

"Oh no," Bradley said, rising to his feet himself. "No, no, no. I can't leave any of this here."

Jennings nodded soberly. "My expenses are top secret, are they?" he said, desperately trying not to laugh in the other man's face.

"No, not top secret by any means," Bradley said, gathering the file up again. "But we have a policy against it."

"Ah, yes," Jennings said, nodding his head. "Where would we be without our policies."

"Exactly," Bradley answered. "I'm glad you understand."

Jennings couldn't resist saying, "Better than you know, Keith."

The comment brought another confused look to the flabby face. Bradley had the file and expense form in his hand, hugging them to his chest. The gesture was effeminate, and reminded Jennings of a high-school girl carrying her books down the hall between classes.

"I'll be back in the morning," the overweight bureaucrat said. "We'll go over it all then."

"I'll look forward to it," Jennings said, again affecting his poker face. He looked down at the trench coat over his arm and suddenly decided to wear it instead of carrying it. He slid his arms into the sleeves, then looked up at Bradley and added,

"Nothing like spending a few hundred dollars in taxpayers' money trying to find a dollar eighty-seven."

Bradley's frown deepened for a moment. Then the man turned and waddled out of the office to disappear around a corner down the hall.

Jennings tied the belt of his trench coat around his waist. At least I dress like a super spy, he thought as he walked out the door. He used his key to drop the dead bolt in place, then started toward the elevators at the end of the hall.

In his mind, he was already at the Shamrock Tavern, three blocks away. He needed a drink. In fact, he needed several drinks. What he needed, Carl Jennings realized as he pushed the elevator button and stared up at the numbers above the door, was however many drinks it would take to get past the point of knowing that his entire career was turning out to be a very bitter disappointment.

4

Bolan turned onto the gravel outside the Fredericksburg Police Department's Air Division building. Guiding the rental car into a parking space, he killed the engine and opened the door. As he did, a man dressed in the full uniform of a color guard walked up holding a clipboard. His name tag read Weston.

"You must be Agent Belasko," Officer Weston said, extending his hand. "Justice Department told us you were on your way."

Bolan grasped the hand and nodded.

"Sorry to bother you with this, sir," Weston said. "But I'll have to see some ID."

The Executioner nodded again. "No bother at all," he said. "Fact is, I'd be tempted to report you to your chief if you didn't ask for it." Pulling his credentials out of a pocket in his leather jacket, he handed them to the man.

The full-dress cop glanced at the picture, back up to Bolan's face, then handed the case back. "Gotta be you." He smiled.

Bolan nodded. "Couldn't be two faces like that in this world, could there?"

"Hey, I didn't say that." Weston laughed. He pointed to a

Jeep Cherokee parked a few spaces from Bolan's car and said, "Hop in. I'll take you down to your ride."

The Executioner got into the passenger's seat of the Jeep as Weston slid behind the wheel. A few seconds later, they passed a hangar that housed a small Piper Cub and three helicopters. All had been painted blue and white and sported the emblem of the Fredericksburg PD on the doors. Painted across the baggage compartments in bold black letters was the word POLICE.

The Learjet was warmed up and waiting at the end of the runway and, through the windshield, Bolan could see Jack Grimaldi at the controls. Weston insisted on shaking hands again as he smiled and said, "Just curious, Cooper, but can you tell me where you're going? Or would you have to kill me then?"

The Executioner chuckled. "I wouldn't have to kill you, but it might bore you to death. Turns out I'm being called as a witness on a tax fraud case I worked with the IRS."

Weston's head bobbed up and down. "You're right," he said. "Don't tell me any more." He grinned wider to make sure Bolan knew he was joking. "And here I was thinking I had a real live supersleuth on my hands."

The Executioner shook his head. "Not me," he said.

Weston held his smile but looked disappointed. Justice Agent Matthew Cooper wasn't turning out to be the romantic character he'd imagined.

When he finally got away, Bolan took his luggage into the cabin with him and stowed it behind the seat next to the pilot. As Grimaldi revved the engine and they began streaking down the runway, he pulled the three money belts out of a bag and laid them on the deck. "Take these back to the Farm when you go, Jack," he said. "Some of the papers are the same, but others are different. And who knows what magic our forensic boys may be able to work?"

"Gotcha, big guy," Grimaldi said as he left the runway and took them airborne.

"Good thing they got word to you in time about Missouri," Bolan said as he settled back into his seat. "We could have found ourselves stuck here with a helicopter."

Grimaldi glanced at his wristwatch as he leveled the plane off in the air. "That would have cut it close, all right," he said. "We'd probably had to have stolen a plane."

Bolan nodded. "Wouldn't be the first time, would it?" he said.

Grimaldi smiled beneath his suede Alaskan bush pilot's cap. "No, sir," he said. "And it probably won't be the last, either."

Since Barbara Price had arranged for a car to be ready and waiting, Bolan had nothing more to do until they arrived in Springfield. If Price or Brognola came up with anything he needed to know, they'd call or get him on the radio.

The Executioner settled back against the seat and closed his eyes. Long years of experience had taught him that a warrior on a mission got little rest, and the wise warrior took what he could get, when he could get it.

The next thing he knew, Jack Grimaldi was shaking his shoulder and saying, "Wake up, Sarge. We're here."

THE BULBS ATOP THE POLES along the street, and the neon signs in the store windows, guided the Executioner to the parking lot of the world-famous Bass Pro Shop in Springfield, Missouri. Four vehicles—all parked close to the main entrance—

stood in the parking area of the giant retail outlet as he passed. He had to assume they belonged to custodians or night security personnel.

Bolan took the next right turn he came to and pulled the rented Nissan Maxima in behind a gas station. Killing the headlights, he let the engine continue to purr as he glanced around the immediate area. Satisfied that his approach had not been observed, he twisted the key in the ignition and the Nissan died into the same silence that surrounded the business area where the shop was located.

Bolan lifted his wrist to his eyes. The luminous dial of his watch read 0416.

He had less than four hours to recon the area, take his best educated guesses as to where the sniper planned to set up, then find a countersniper "hide" of his own. It wouldn't be easy.

The Executioner opened the door. His first action upon taking possession of the Nissan had been to disconnect the dome light, and the car remained dark as he stepped out of the car. He was wearing a baggy blue work shirt and khaki pants two sizes too large. The garments were quickly shed to reveal his combat blacksuit and weapons.

Tossing the cover shirt and pants over the seat into the back, Bolan quietly closed the door and moved toward the back of the gas station. Keeping to the shadows, the Executioner made his way to the front of the building. The sign in the window announced that the business would reopen at 0600, which meant he had roughly an hour and a half before he'd have to move the Nissan. He wanted the blacksuit for cover as he moved about the area in the night. But the sun would have risen by the time employees began arriving, and showing up in full battle gear to grab his car would accomplish nothing but phone calls to the Springfield PD.

Just as before, the local cops could do nothing to help him. But their good intentions could cause any number of problems to arise. And if they had any suspicions from their own intelligence sources that a sniper attack was planned, the responding officers would more than likely consider him an enemy rather than an ally. He would keep to himself, as usual.

The Executioner let a pickup truck pass by the station and waited until its red taillights had faded in the distance before sprinting across the street to a shopping center. He continued to move through the shadows then darted across a side street into the Bass parking lot. Squatting behind a sign, he surveyed the area once more. No one had taken notice of him, and he rose back to his feet and raced toward the main entrance of the store.

Bolan's rubber-soled nylon combat boots left the asphalt of the parking lot and hit the concrete sidewalk leading up to the doorway. He avoided the lights by taking cover behind a row of bushes. The main entrance was well-lit, and he'd be highly visible during the time he spent in the area—not just to curious eyes but to the sniper himself if the man had already set up.

He knew he'd have to minimize that time as best he could.

Bolan waited in the shadows, still watching the night for any sign that he'd been seen. The Bass Pro Shop had several entrances but the main door was the one that interested him. More translations had come through during his flight to Missouri, and they made it clear that the al Qaeda target would be entering and exiting at this spot. According to the papers he'd found in the money belts, the Pro Shop Café, which opened earlier than the rest of the store, lay just beyond this entryway.

Bolan, however, wanted to look through the glass and confirm that fact himself. He had worked too many missions to trust advance intelligence completely.

Looking out over the top of the bushes, he could see he was only a foot or two from where the mayor of Springfield would soon walk up the steps for his daily breakfast. Shifting his eyes, the Executioner scouted the area in the distance for potential sniper hides.

Bolan realized there were far too many places for a sniper to set up in the tall buildings that formed a semicircle around the entryway. There was no way he could possibly cover them all. To try would be futility at its worst.

Rather than run up the steps to the front door, Bolan rose, reached overhead to grasp the railing at the side of the steps and hauled himself up to the landing. He was still in the shadows and, he hoped, invisible to anyone looking down though a spotter's scope from a window or other secluded area in the distance.

Bolan scanned the buildings in the distance one last time. Then, keeping low, he hurried to the doors and squatted next to the glass. In less than a second's time he saw the tables just past the entryway, the chairs upended and set upon the tabletops. An elderly man was sweeping the floor with a large dust mop, and just behind him the Executioner could see a swing door that had to lead to the kitchen.

Convinced that he was at the right doorway, Bolan wasted no more time in the open. In a heartbeat he had pivoted back around on the balls of his feet, hurried back to the steps and dived over the railing back into the bushes.

The Executioner landed on his shoulder in the dirt behind the waist-high plants, rolled forward and came up on one knee. Yet again, his eyes darted out and across the buildings in front of the Pro Shop. And again, there was no indication that he'd been seen.

The Executioner glanced at his watch again. Creeping to the building in the darkness had taken almost forty-five minutes. He had no time to lose—to the east, he could see the black night lightening to the gray of dawn.

Staying low, Bolan hurried to the end of the bushes, then sprinted back across the street. A few minutes later he had arrived back behind the service station. Opening the trunk of the Nissan, he pulled out a black plastic hard case and a Kevlar vest, then softly closed the trunk again. Sliding behind the wheel, he set the case and vest next to him in the passenger's seat, fired up the engine and pulled out onto the street.

The enormous number of potential sniper sights had meant a drastic change in strategy and Bolan putting his new plan into effect by pulling into the parking lot of the Bass Pro Shop. There was no way he could cover every window and other hiding place from which the al Qaeda man might fire. He decided to work back the other way, making sure that the mayor was not hit, and then doing his best to pinpoint the sniper area from shots fired.

The same four cars that had been there earlier were still in the lot as the Executioner pulled the Maxima to a halt two spaces away from a ten-year-old Oldsmobile. From the driver's seat, he had a clear view of the main entrance. But sitting behind the wheel dressed as he was would raise some eyebrows when café customers and employees began arriving. He needed to do something about that, and he needed to do it before anyone else arrived in the parking lot.

Quickly, Bolan slid into the bullet-resistant vest, then reached into the back seat for the blue work shirt he'd discarded earlier. He stuck his arms into the sleeves to conceal his shoulder rig but left it unbuttoned to access the Beretta. Unless someone looked closely, the vest would appear to be a T-shirt worn underneath the open shirt.

Bolan paused, looking over the seat at the khaki pants. The car covered him below the waist, and the tail of his shirt was long enough to hide the Desert Eagle and other gear at his waist even when he got out of the car. But his new plan included going inside the store, and with the black legs of the combat suit sticking out below the shirt, he'd look like he was wearing a leotard. A hard smile curled the Executioner's lips as he pulled the pants over the seat, then struggled them up over his legs beneath the steering wheel. A man wearing a leotard might not draw much attention in San Francisco or Greenwich Village but this was Springfield, Missouri. Here, men dressed, and acted, like men.

With shirt and pants now in place, the Executioner flipped the latches of the hard case next to him, opened the lid and reached inside to the Calico 950.

Then he settled back to play the role of early-morning customer waiting for the Bass Pro Shop to open.

5

The Executioner remained behind the wheel of the Maxima as a dilapidated Chevy pickup turned off the street into the lot in the early dawn light. The blown-out muffler roared as the driver turned the vehicle into one of the spaces marked Employees Only at the rear of the parking lot. A moment after the truck had ground to a halt, an elderly man wearing a security guard uniform got out and began limping across the concrete toward the main entrance. He passed the hood of the Nissan without a glance inside, and Bolan watched him hobble past the Oldsmobile, then up the steps to the store's main entrance. The old man used his arms on the handrail as much as his legs as he pulled himself toward the door.

Two men who looked like janitors came out of the building as the old man reached the top step. Nods were exchanged, then the night custodians both stopped to light cigarettes as the elderly guard disappeared inside. As soon as the smoke began rising from both of their mouths, they hurried down the steps and drove away in two of the automobiles parked in the lot.

The janitors had barely driven away when a college-aged kid in a security uniform similar to the old man's came bounding out the front door and down the steps. In one arm, he carried what looked like several textbooks. With a hurried glance at his wristwatch, he left the parking lot in a rattling relic of what had once been a gold 1965 Dodge Dart GT. Bolan watched him already unbuttoning his uniform blouse as he drove away, evidently headed toward an early class.

Except for the elderly security guard's car at the rear of the lot, and the Executioner's Nissan, the only vehicle left was the Oldsmobile.

As the gray morning grew lighter around Bolan, more employees began arriving, parking at the back of the lot and walking across the asphalt. Bolan glanced at his watch again—0645. According to the sign he had seen in the window the night before, the café area would open at 0700 with the store itself following two hours later.

According to the translation of the papers Bolan had found in the al Qaeda money belts, the Honorable Rupert Q. Choate, mayor of Springfield, would be driven to the front door at precisely 0730. Choate was known to be a creature of habit; he would exit the city-owned Lincoln Town Car, enter the building, and breakfast on scrambled eggs, sausage and two pieces of toast. He would exit again at precisely 0800 and be driven to his office in the city government building downtown. Choate's only divergence from this routine was the occasional guest he sometimes met at the Pro Shop Café for breakfast.

And, according to the al Qaeda intel, this morning Missouri Senator Dwight Appleby would be joining him.

The sun had risen high enough to illuminate the area, and the Executioner twisted slightly, looking out of the Nissan's passenger window to again scan the buildings in the distance. His trained and practiced eye moved left to right, then right to left. His mind painted imaginary stripes from the car out over the horizon and he scanned up and down, in and out.

Bolan knew there was no way he could take out the sniper before he fired. He would be forced to rely on his quickly devised alternate plan: Get out of the Nissan a few minutes before 0800, enter the store and walk out with Choate and Appleby. He would then get in front of them and knock both men out of the line of fire as the sniper pulled the trigger.

If he was lucky, he might be able to pinpoint the sniper's hide then. If not, at least he would keep the men alive.

Three more cars pulled into the lot a few minutes before 0700 and parked in the employees area. One man and two women, all wearing the aprons of cooks and waitresses, walked swiftly past the Executioner and mounted the steps. The traffic on the street continued to thicken as the Springfield, Missouri, workforce headed to their jobs.

A few more early-morning breakfasters and coffee drinkers arrived shortly before 0730. As customers, they parked as close to the doorway as possible, completely encircling Bolan's Nissan and the Oldsmobile still parked next to him. Most of the drivers stayed in their vehicles, waiting and periodically glancing at their wrists. One man, wearing olive green work pants and a matching shirt with a name tag over the left breast, got out of his car, mounted the concrete steps and tried the door. Finding it still locked, he took a seat on the top step to wait.

Bolan's wristwatch read exactly 0729 when the Lincoln Town Car pulled into the parking lot from a side street and drove slowly toward the entrance. The vehicle stopped directly in front of the door, and the Executioner saw a man wearing a dark suit and chauffeur's cap behind the wheel. He got out, walked around the hood and opened the back door.

A man in his midsixties, wearing a silver-gray suit with hair that almost matched, stepped out. The chauffeur closed the door, then hurried back around the Lincoln to the driver's side and pulled the vehicle to a parking space near Bolan's.

Inside the Bass Pro Shop, on the other side of the glass door, Bolan saw a white-aproned employee unlock the door and hold it back. The employee had evidently been waiting for the mayor.

Suddenly car doors opened, slammed shut, and the rest of the people who had been waiting for the café to open began walking toward the door. Mayor Choate was not only a creature of habit but a creature who obviously reveled in his position. He had strutted up the steps with a gait more befitting a king than the mayor of a midsize city in the Midwest, and the Executioner suspected all hell would have broken loose had the employee not been there to unlock the door at exactly the right time.

Less than five minutes later a light brown Ford pickup arrived and parked in the space directly across from the Executioner. The driver wore a wide-brimmed cowboy hat and, for a brief moment, his eyes met Bolan's. Then he opened his door, got out and turned toward the café. Bolan waited until the man was halfway to the steps before tapping numbers into the cell phone.

Price answered on the second ring. "Good morning, Striker. Have a nice night?"

"Fantastic," the Executioner said. "You have a description for me on Senator Appleby yet?"

"Hang on," Price said. "Let me check with Bear."

Bolan waited. Not that he really needed a description. The man in the cowboy hat and Choate might as well have had Politician branded on each of their chests. But there was no reason to take chances when you didn't have to.

Twenty seconds later, Price was back on the line. "Fifty-five years old, salt-and pepper hair, five-foot-seven and about thirty pounds overweight. Likes to dress Western when he's at home but wears Brooks Brothers on the Senate floor."

"What's he drive?" Bolan asked, to be certain.

"Just a second," Price said. This time, he heard her tapping her own keyboard keys. Getting registration for any and all vehicles registered in the senator's name was mere child's play. It could be done by simply linking into the Department of Motor Vehicles in Missouri and D.C. "There's about five . . . no six vehicles registered under his name," the Stony Man mission controller said a moment later. On the other end of the connection, Bolan heard her laugh softly.

"Something funny?" he asked.

"Yeah," Price said. "It's like the way he dresses one way in Washington, another at home. Two Mercedes and a Caddie registered in Washington. In Missouri, though, he's one of the boys. A Dodge Ram Van and two pickups."

"Tell me about the pickups."

"One Ford, one Chevy," Price said.

"What color's the Ford?"

"Tan."

The Executioner nodded. Light brown, beige, tan—call it what you wanted. It was the senator's truck sitting across from him, and the man in the cowboy had was Dwight Appleby. "Thanks, Barb," the Executioner said. He was about to disconnect when he heard Price take a deep breath.

"It's getting close to show time," she said. "You got the sniper spotted?"

"No," Bolan said. "Too many places he could be." He paused, knowing what he was about to say would bother the woman on the other end of the line. On the other hand, it would bother her only for a second. Barbara Price—like the Executioner himself—was far too professional to let personal feelings get in the way of a mission.

Bolan and Price had had more than a passing interest in each other since the first day she'd taken up her role as mission controller for Stony Man Farm. But with Bolan on the road most of the time, doing what he did, both knew it was a relationship that could never blossom into anything even vaguely resembling a normal love affair. So they accepted it for what it was, made it all it could be, and never pretended it could ever become anything more.

"I'll have to work it from the other end," the Executioner said. "I'll have to get between the sniper and Choate and Appleby, then do my best to knock all three of us out of the way right before the shot."

There was a long pause on the other end of the line. "How are you going to know when the shot's coming?" Price asked.

"Hunch," the Executioner replied. "Instinct. And experience. If I were the shooter, I'd wait until they got to the bottom of the steps. That's the natural place for them to stop, shake hands, and say their goodbyes."

"And if you're wrong?" Price demanded to know.

"Then I take a bullet," Bolan said matter-of-factly. "But if

I'm right, my guess is the sniper will immediately fire again." He paused and drew in a breath, his eyes moving to the bottom of the concrete steps leading up into the store. "It's hard to pinpoint the sound of one shot. Much easier when somebody shoots twice."

"And then what?" Price asked.

"I go after him."

"That's thin."

"Yes," Bolan agreed. "It is. But it's all I've got."

There was another long pause, then Stony Man Farm's mission controller spoke again. "You've got your vest?" she asked.

The Executioner smiled. Price was remaining professionally detached as usual. But beneath her tone was the barest hint of concern.

"Vest's on," Bolan said. "Steel plate inserted over the heart."

"Good," Price replied. The faint undertone had vanished. "Anything else you need from this end?"

"Nope."

"Affirmative, " Price said. "Stony Man out." She hung up.

The Executioner killed the call on his end and clipped the phone back to his belt. He glanced at his watch. 0755.

Five minutes and counting. The mayor and his breakfast guest would be exiting the Bass Pro Shop café in exactly five minutes. It was time Bolan got inside himself so he could walk out with them.

The Executioner lifted the Calico 950 submachine pistol out of the hard case. Attached on the top of the weapon was a 50-round drum magazine filled with 9 mm rounds. A 100-round backup drum had already been inserted into the carry pocket of the shoulder rig for the weapon. It was long and cumbersome, and would be difficult to conceal beneath the light work shirt. He left it in place as the fingers of his right hand curled around the grip, then tucked the weapon out of sight under his left arm beside the Beretta.

Bolan's hand fell to the door handle. He was about to open the door when a sudden flash of movement in the Oldsmobile next to him froze him in place. He had been seated next to the empty car for almost two hours now.

But now, suddenly, he realized it had not been empty.

Less than three feet away from the Executioner, four heads suddenly rose above the windows. The loose tails of kaffiyehs drifted down around the faces of the men. The quartet turned to face the Maxima.

The barrels of two Uzis, a Heckler & Koch MP-5, and what looked like an AK-74 with a folding stock appeared through the window glass.

For a brief second, time seemed to stand still, and during that second Bolan sized up the situation. Just as the Executioner had altered his own plan of attack to meet the situation, al Qaeda had changed tactics. Instead of a sniper setting up in the distance as outlined in the pages found in their money belts, whoever was in charge of this strike had made a change. The strategy had gone from a lone sniper to four heavily armed men who would simply blast their way into the café, murder the mayor, the senator and probably everyone else inside.

Then, they would blast their way back out again. They could easily be gone before the police arrived. Or, they might stay and fight it out with the cops, too.

Bolan knew the same mentality that motivated suicide

bombers could easily be transferred to submachine guns and assault rifles.

The barrels of the weapons were trained on the Nissan.

The Executioner realized the terrorists had known he was next to them from the moment he'd parked. They had probably watched him recon the café. They had kept out of sight beneath the Oldsmobile's windows, but had been aware of his presence—and were preparing to kill him first—all along.

Bolan knew the only reason they hadn't killed him already was because they were waiting for Choate and Appleby to arrive; if they started the shooting too early, police would respond and the ensuing gunfight with the boys in blue would have sidetracked them from their primary mission.

With the Calico still gripped in his right fist, Bolan dived down and grabbed for the passenger door's handle with his left. As he did, automatic gunfire began chattering from the Oldsmobile, and 9 mm and .223 rounds drilled through the Maxima over his head.

The bullets shattered the glass in the windows and windshield, and ground holes through the steel doors and the rest of the Nissan's body.

The Executioner pulled the handle at the same time his head struck the door, forcing it open. He felt something hot slide up his ribs, then scrape skin off his upper arm as he dived out of the car and fell facedown onto the concrete.

Staying low to the ground, Bolan twirled back toward the Nissan as more automatic fire peppered the vehicle. His left hand shot to his right side, tracing the path one of the bullets had taken up his torso and across his right biceps. His fingers came away bloody. But the wound was superficial. It had scoured away far more skin than tissue, and he turned is attention back to the men in the Oldsmobile.

The people in the parking lot, on their way into the store, had frozen in place at the first sounds of the gunfire. Now, seconds later, many had had time to process what was going on, and react. Those reactions ranged from screams, cries and running, to continuing to stand in place like stone statues.

For a second, the gunfire ceased and, above the shrieks of terror, the Executioner heard the sounds of car doors opening. Although he had yet to fire his first round, the al Qaeda men obviously knew, or at least suspected, that they had not yet put him out of the fight. They were too smart to stay bunched up together in the vehicle where they'd be easy to take out all at once. The men had seen Bolan operate as he reconned the building, and they had watched his reflexes and lightning-like escape from the Nissan as soon as their assault had begun. They might not know exactly who he was. But they knew what he was. A pro who had come to stop them.

Two pairs of feet appeared on the other side of the Nissan as the men on Bolan's side got out of the front and back seat. Both wore blue jeans and white athletic shoes. The Executioner pointed the Calico at the ankles of the man to his right and pulled the trigger. A full-auto burst of semijacketed 9 mm hollowpoint rounds shot beneath the Maxima's chassis and into his target. A yelp sounded between the rounds, and as he let up on the trigger Bolan heard the yelp turn to a squeal of anguish. The man dropped to his knees on the other side of the car, his feet and ankles almost nonexistent.

Bolan swung the Calico slightly to his left, ready to squeeze the trigger once more and do the same to the man emerging from the back seat. But as he did, the terrorist's feet seemed to disappear. The Executioner heard the dull thump on the roof of the Nissan and knew what had happened.

The al Qaeda man from the back seat of the Oldsmobile had leaped up onto the Maxima. He planned to come over the top of the car and kill Bolan from above.

Leaning onto his left side, the Executioner angled the Calico's barrel up through the shattered glass of the window above him. He held the trigger back, sending a stream of full-auto fire through the roof of the vehicle. The gray sky of the early-morning sun appeared through all but one of the holes as the 9 mm rounds drilled through the thin metal. The hole at the far rear of the roof remained dark. And a moment later, drops of crimson rain began to fall onto the seats within the car.

More shrill screeches of pain rose as the man on top of the Nissan slid across the roof through his own blood. He fell onto Bolan. The Executioner pushed the dead man aside.

Rolling back to his belly on the concrete, Bolan aimed the Calico beneath the Maxima once more and sent another blast of fire into the thighs of the terrorist still upright on his knees. The new rounds tore through his quadriceps and hamstrings, tearing muscle and severing ligaments and tendons and forcing him forward onto his hands as well as his knees. With his head and most of his chest still out of sight above the Nissan, Bolan sent another burst of fire to shatter the man's elbows. The al Qaeda killer fell on down to the side of his face. For a moment, the wild eyes of the hate-filled zealot stared at the Executioner beneath the Nissan.

Another barrage from the Calico obliterated those eyes, as well as the hatred shooting forth from them.

The Executioner rose to his knees behind the Maxima. As the explosions from the Calico died down the screams all around him in the parking lot became audible. Bolan heard running footsteps behind him, and turned just in time to see a well-meaning but confused man wearing a Missouri State Football letter jacket leave his feet in a flying tackle. Shifting to the side, Bolan let the man pass by.

The crew-cut head above the thickly muscled neck struck the Nissan's door, leaving a dent the size of a cantaloupe in the metal. But the football player got the worst of the deal, knocking himself cold and preventing the Executioner from having to do that job himself.

Rising slightly above the window, Bolan's eyes searched for the other two terrorists. They had left the Oldsmobile on the far side, but he had heard no gunfire from either of them during the seconds that had transpired. He caught a quick glimpse of the AK-74 he had seen earlier, and ducked back down just in time to avoid a 3-round burst of .223 rounds, which sailed over his head.

Excited shouts in Arabic flew through the air as the gunfire died down again. Crabbing his way toward the front of the quickly disintegrating Nissan, Bolan took refuge behind the engine block, then slowly peered around the front bumper. The remaining two al Qaeda men had taken off running, and were nearing the top of the steps leading into the main entrance. As he swung the Calico in front of him to fire, the door suddenly opened and the elderly security guard the Executioner had watched arrive at work that very morning stepped out. The old man held a .38 Special revolver in his trembling hands.

The Executioner dropped the Calico's sights on the back

of the terrorist with the AK-74. He'd started to squeeze the trigger when the security guard stepped directly behind his target. The Executioner let up on the trigger, fearing his own penetrating 9 mm rounds would drill through the terrorist and into the old man. But his caution proved futile. Even as he relaxed his trigger finger, the al Qaeda killer twisted at the waist and sent a burst of fire from his Uzi into the guard.

The old man fell to the ground and lay still.

Bolan's jaw set tight as he redirected his aim at the terrorist with the Uzi. But by the time he had sighted the target in, both terrorists had disappeared through the door into the Bass Pro Shop.

Rising, the Executioner sprinted toward the steps, silently praying that Mayor Choate and Senator Appleby had heard the gunfire in the parking lot, realized they had to be the reason behind it, and had the common sense to find a hiding place somewhere within the gigantic retail outlet. If they could stay out of sight long enough for Bolan to track the al Qaeda men, they might yet survive.

The Executioner reached the top of the steps and jumped over the body of the dead security guard. There was nothing he could do for the old man.

Landing on the concrete on the other side of the corpse, Bolan jerked the door open and raced into the Pro Shop's front entryway. Bullets sailed over the Executioner's head as he dived forward onto the floor just inside the door. Behind him, he heard the crash of glass doors and windows breaking into pieces. Huge chunks fell to the floor, shattering against the hard tiles and sending thousands of sparkling shards cascading through the area.

Bolan looked up to see the café area directly ahead of him. Choate and Appleby were not seated at any of the tables. No one was seated at any of the tables. But he saw no bodies on the floor so he could still hope that the gunfire in the parking lot had given the patrons sufficient time to go into hiding.

But the al Qaeda men had gone into hiding too.

The gunfire had come from Bolan's right, however, and he slid along the tile in that direction. Ignoring the small cuts and stabs from the broken glass through which he moved, the soldier made his way toward a steel railing that separated the entryway from a huge overhead sign that read Boats. On the other side of the rail, filling the showroom, he could see fishing boats, and other craft of all makes and models. One giant power cruiser hung from the ceiling on sturdy iron chains. Beneath it were shelves of plastic-wrapped inflatable dinghies, and to the side of the shelves a portable wooden staircase that led up into the air so potential buyers could inspect the cruiser's deck and cabin.

Bolan waited, letting his ears continue to clear. As they did, he heard whispers somewhere ahead among the vessels.

In Arabic.

Bolan moved along the rail, then through the opening into the showroom. When he reached the suspended cabin cruiser, he crouched at the foot of the wooden steps. The whispers were louder.

Bolan leaned slowly around the side of the steps toward the muffled voices. But the men doing the whispering had heard him, too. The whispers suddenly stopped and were replaced with more roars from the Uzi and AK-74. Bullets struck the steps, drilling holes through the wood, and sending splinters and paint chips flying through the air like shrapnel.

The Executioner threw himself forward, hitting the ground on his side and rolling behind the hull of a light fishing boat. But the boat was mere concealment rather than cover, and he was forced to roll on as the gunfire followed him, blowing holes the size of fists through the thin aluminum. Scrambling across the tile, Bolan dived to the side of a small catamaran sailboat. But the twin plastic hulls were no more bullet-repellant than the aluminum, and were quickly spotted with perforations. Unable to pause even for breath, Bolan lunged back in the direction from which he'd come, passing the wooden steps again before finally ducking out of sight behind the shelves beneath the suspended cabin cruiser. Blocked from the terrorists' view by stacks of deflated and folded rubber dinghies, the Executioner hugged the ground as rifle and submachine gun fire pelted the shelves, sending a rainstorm of rubber and plastic falling down over him.

The gunfire ended abruptly as the al Qaeda men realized their target had disappeared. An eerie silence fell over the showroom. Then the sound of running footsteps could be heard in the distance.

Bolan leaped to his feet, clutching the Calico in his right hand. Sprinting after the footsteps, he passed row after row of boats and water sports equipment. His own boots drowned out the sounds of the footfalls ahead of him, and he knew each successive boat, or row of shelves, might hide the terrorists. The al Qaeda men could just as easily have stopped for an ambush as continued running.

But the Executioner had no choice but to chance it. The terrorists were not about to give up their mission. They had come to assassinate Mayor Choate and Senator Appleby, and

Bolan knew that even as they fled from him they searched for the hiding politicians.

Curling his left hand around and under his armpit, the Executioner drew the sound-suppressed Beretta 93-R and flipped the selector switch to 3-round burst. As he raced on, he kept his eyes straight ahead down the aisle, relying on his peripheral vision to alert him to any surprises that might be waiting for him behind the obstacles he passed. With the Calico, he covered his right. With the Beretta, his left.

Bolan still wore the Kevlar vest, but it hardly made him invincible. While the tightly woven fabric would probably stop the 9 mm rounds from the Uzi it would be next to worthless against the penetrating .223 bullets from the AK-74. The steel plate inserted into the pocket over his heart might stop such rounds—as long as he was struck head-on. But if enemy rifle fire came from the sides, it would bypass the steel and drill through the Kevlar as if it were not even there. Even the 9 mm subgun fire might find its mark through the arm holes or between the side closures of the vest. And nothing would protect the Executioner from gunfire below the waist or to the head.

His knees pumping high with each step, Bolan suddenly passed a cabin cruiser and caught a glimpse of movement to his left. His trigger finger squeezed back on the Beretta in reflex even as he heard the rounds from the AK-74 explode in his ears.

The Executioner knew he could not outrun bullets. But moving at full speed as he was, he outran both his own and the al Qaeda killer's reaction time. The .223 rounds from the assault rifle ripped past him an inch behind his back. His own quietly coughing 9 mm rounds also missed their target by a fraction of an inch.

Bolan was past the man lying in wait before either he or the terrorist could fire again.

Turning his right foot sideways on the tile, the Executioner dipped a shoulder and performed a three-point turn like an NFL linebacker suddenly changing direction. Pivoting back toward the cruiser, he heard the stutter of the Uzi from somewhere deeper in the boat area. More rounds flew past him from behind.

Caught in a crossfire between the two al Qaeda men, the Executioner dived down the side aisle to his right, and took refuge between the hulls of two flat day-sailers. Again, the boats offered no cover and precious little concealment, and as rifle and submachine ground rounds stippled the craft and everything around it, Bolan was forced to roll on.

He came to a halt on his belly, facing back toward the spot where he had last seen the terrorist. Aiming the Calico through the thin plastic side of the day-sailer between them, he held the trigger back and sent a steady stream of fire ripping blindly through the boat.

He had directed the volley at the terrorist more as a deterrent than a killing assault, hoping it would allow him to move on to better cover. But, sometimes, Lady Luck smiled on the Executioner, and he heard a loud scream.

Bolan rose quickly in response to the sound. On the floor, less than five feet away on the other side of the boat, he saw the man with the AK-74. At least half of the Executioner's rounds looked as if they'd found the terrorist, and the majority of those appeared to have struck the killer's head.

More fire from behind him forced Bolan back to the floor. As he fell, he felt another round rip through the blue work shirt. Not that his cover garments were serving any useful purpose anymore—any low profile they had provided earlier had gone out the window with the first shot. They were nothing but a hindrance to his movements so he rolled to one side on the tile, shrugged out of the opposite sleeve of the shirt, then rolled back the other way and let the shirt fall to the tile. Taking off the khaki pants in the conventional manner would have put him in a temporarily compromised position. So instead of struggling them down over his boots, he drew the knife from behind his back and sliced the trousers from the waistband down both legs. The khakis fell away.

Clad now in the combat blacksuit, the Kevlar vest exposed over it, the Executioner waited while more Uzi rounds kept him hugging the floor. When the subgun stopped a second later he heard the patter of running footsteps again. How far away they might be, or in what direction they were moving, he couldn't tell. The almost continuous explosions that had assaulted his eardrums for the last five minutes had taken their toll.

Bolan sheathed the knife, picked up the Calico from the floor, rose to his feet and took off in the direction from which he knew the shots had come. Ahead, he could see the back wall of the boating area, and a sign announcing OUTDOOR WEAR with an arrow pointing to his left. He followed the main aisle until it turned in the direction of the arrow, and suddenly found himself surrounded by row after row of stacked hunting pants, jeans, thick woolen shirts and other clothing. Backing up against a circular rack of insulated tree-bark camou field shirts, he listened again.

Nothing. Once again, the Bass Pro Shop had taken on the silence of a tomb.

Bolan waited, his senses on alert as his mind raced to cover all aspects of the current battle. The mayor and senator had to be hidden somewhere inside the store. But they were smart enough to keep quiet. So were the café staff, and the other employees who had arrived before official opening hours. That was good.

But the final terrorist was remaining quiet, too. And that was bad.

The Executioner moved forward slowly. A store such as this had literally thousands of nooks and crannies large enough to hide a man. It was as much jungle as retail outlet, he realized, as he stalked cautiously on. Each circular rack of jackets sprouting up from the floor might as well have been a thickly leaved tree in the middle of the Amazon. Every stack of shelves was a rise in the topography behind which the al Qaeda killer might crouch as if it were a hilly area within a rain forest. The shirts, pants and other items of clothing that hung from the bars mounted along the walls were no different than hanging jungle vines. The terrorist could have hidden himself within any of them. He could be watching, waiting, biding his time until the Executioner unwittingly moved across the sights of his Uzi. It had become a game of patience and stealth.

And the first man to make a mistake would die.

Bolan continued to move silently along the tile, sliding in a combat crouch, an inch at a time. He stayed close to the sides of the aisles where the clothing offered some concealment. Gradually, he made his way out of the shirts and pants to an area filled with heavy woolen overcoats, parkas and rain-repellent outerwear. As the roar in his ears continued to die down, he paused each time he heard a sound, his eyes darting toward the direction from which it came, either the Beretta or Calico or both following a split second later. But none of the noises proved relevant to the death hunt at hand.

Beyond the coat area, the Executioner saw that the entire back wall of that side of the store was devoted to boots and shoes. Between the last rack of coats and the wall was a large open space where benches had been placed so customers could sit to try on the footwear.

Bolan stopped just short of the final coat rack. Quickly, he scanned the open area. The benches offered no concealment. The man he sought had not hidden there.

Still crouched low, the Executioner felt the burn in his thigh muscles. He ignored it. Turning his attention to the side, he began making his way between two huge tables scattered with stacks of discounted T-shirts and sweatshirts.

Beyond the tables, another open area led to the staircase to the basement floor. A sign above the stairs announced that by descending the steps the customer would find himself amid the Hunting, Fishing, Camping and Team Sports departments. Two other, smaller, signs—one featuring the stick figure of a man, the other a similar figure clad in a dress—pointed the way toward rest rooms.

Bolan came to the end of the display tables and stopped, listening. The store remained silent. But as soon as he moved out and away from cover the roar of subgun chatter exploded against the walls once more.

For a moment, the Executioner felt as if a train had driven along its tracks and into his chest. Then a second train hit, and a third, and the three concussions sent him sailing back between the tables. T-shirts and sweatshirts of all colors tumbled down to cover him as more automatic fire blasted above a strange clanging sound. Beneath the scattered T-shirts, the Executioner felt a vibration against his chest.

It took Bolan a brief moment to come back to his senses. But when he did, he looked down and saw that two of the 9 mm rounds had penetrated the first three layers of his tightly woven Kevlar. One of the now-distorted hollow point rounds still clung to the vest, its jagged edges trapped in the fabric. The third round had hit him squarely over the heart. It had struck the steel insert and ricocheted off.

As the vibrations settled, the Executioner swept the fallen shirts to the side and looked out across the open area in time to see a man in a kaffiyeh descending the steps to the lower floor.

Bolan leaped to his feet and ran after the man. The vest had saved his life, but his torso felt as if the cleanup hitter for a big league baseball team had taken batting practice beneath it. Flames shot down his body from the spots where the bullets had impacted, following the nerve routes all the way down his legs and into his feet. Again, he pushed the pain to the back of his mind and forced one foot ahead of the other.

The Executioner stopped at the top of the stairs. He holstered the Beretta and aimed the Calico downward. The open stairway was a death trap. He'd not only be spotlighted from the front and sides, but the al Qaeda gunner could shoot between the steps from the rear as well. But he had no choice. He had to get down the steps, and there was no time to search for an alternate route down. Somewhere in the store, Mayor Choate, Senator Appleby, and other innocents still hid in terror. If Bolan didn't find the terrorist before the man found them, they would die.

As so often happened in battle, the Executioner's strategy came to him suddenly, and he wasted no time putting it into action. Taking three steps away from the top step, he sprinted forward and leaped into the air, flying out and over the staircase like a broad jumper. He was airborne for less than two seconds—enough time enough for the al Qaeda man's brain to register what was happening and react, but not react accurately. More 9 mm rounds broke the silence just before Bolan's boots hit the floor. But the shots had been hurried, and they sailed behind him with no more damage than if they'd never been fired.

Bolan hit the ground two feet in front of the bottom step and rolled forward between two rows of camping equipment. As another burst of fire exploded one of his boots struck a display stand, and a camp stove fell to the floor, rattling across the tile.

Staying low between the aisles the Executioner let a steady stream of rounds skim harmlessly overhead. Then, rising as high as he dared, he looked behind, trying to get a sense of where the rounds were striking, and from that determine the location from which they came. As bullet holes began appear in a row of battery-operated camp lanterns, he wondered again about the safety of the mayor and the senator.

So far, he'd kept the pressure on the al Qaeda man. The terrorist had been forced to focus on staying alive rather than searching for his prey. But how long would such luck continue? Bolan had lost track of him several times already, not picking up his trail again until more rounds were fired from the Uzi. How long would it be before the man figured out that if he'd just stop shooting, he could slip quietly away, easily losing his pursuer in a store as large as this?

Bolan studied the angle of the holes peppering the camp lanterns and other equipment. When the al Qaeda gunner had time to realize the opportunity he had, he'd take advantage of it. And when he did, there was every chance in the world that he'd find the politicians and kill them.

Round after round continued to pour from the Uzi. It seemed like the al Qaeda man had a bottomless 9 mm magazine. But Bolan knew he didn't, and another plan formed. The magazine had to run dry eventually. The Executioner waited.

The shooting stopped suddenly. Faintly, in the distance, from roughly the same area he had determined from watching the bullet holes, Bolan heard the familiar scraping sound of a box mag being ejected from the grip. To the Executioner, that was as good as a pistol shot at the starting line of a foot race, and he rose to his feet and came out of the blocks at full speed.

Racing toward the sound, Bolan heard the rip of Velcro, and could all but see the terrorist pulling a fresh 30-round mag from its carrier. The noise had come from behind what looked like a waist-level display table of hats.

White linen had been spread across the display table beneath the hats, and it fell down the sides almost to the floor. In the middle of the sheeting, Bolan saw the Bass Pro Shop logo—a leaping fish. Sprinting straight toward the display, he brought the Calico up as the sound of another 9 mm magazine scraped its way into the Uzi. A second later, the white top of the kaffiyeh appeared just above the hat display. Bolan could see it between a cloth safari hat and a leather baseball cap.

The barrel of the Uzi appeared next, and the 9 mm hole in the end stared dully at the Executioner like the gaping black eye-socket of a Cyclops.

The Calico 950 was as good as submachine pistols came, and it had been cared for by Stony Man Farm armorer Cowboy John Kissinger as if it were his own infant child. But no machine was perfect, and even those that were top of the line, even when properly maintained, could fail.

Bolan pointed the submachine pistol at the bearded face between the hats and squeezed the trigger. But instead of the familiar crisp break, followed by an explosion, the trigger moved back a quarter of an inch, then stopped. Turning the weapon slightly to the side and glancing down, he saw the gleaming brass case jammed half-in, half-out of the ejection port at the bottom of the gun.

A stovepipe jam. It had to have happened at the end of his last volley of fire. Bolan had been too busy locating the al Qaeda killer's position to notice it.

What was called a "tap, rack, bang" drill would solve the problem. But as surely as he knew the Calico was jammed, Bolan knew there was no time to clear the empty brass and cycle a fresh round into the chamber. Nor was there time to drop the malfunctioning weapon and reach for either the Beretta or Desert Eagle.

Ten feet from the hat display, still running full speed and unable to slow down, the Executioner saw the al Qaeda killer's fingers tighten around the grip of the Uzi.

6

Carl Jennings walked toward his usual seat at the end of the bar facing the door of the Shamrock Tavern. Sitting with his back to the wall was a habit he had forced himself to acquire years before when he'd first decided to become an intelligence officer. He rarely thought about it any more—it had become second nature to him. But as he slid onto the stool and nodded to the bartender for his usual, it occurred to him that worrying about such things in his present position was a little silly.

Jennings felt his cheeks begin to burn. No one was going to sneak into the Shamrock and shoot him in the back. No one had any reason at all to want him dead. He might work for Homeland Security, but the cold hard fact was that he'd never done a damn thing to help his country or hurt any of its enemies. His stool facing the door was far more like the seat the Norm character always occupied on the TV sitcom *Cheers* than a strategic position from which a spy might defend himself.

Jennings watched as Frank, the new bartender, poured two shots of vodka into a glass, added a touch of vermouth and stirred it with a swizzle stick. He felt himself flush again, remembering the first night Frank had been behind the bar. It had been less than a week ago, and Jennings and several other

Homeland Security drones had already had a few drinks at another place down the street. When the party had broken up there, the Yale man and a couple of others had migrated to the Shamrock, and he'd been just tipsy enough to make a big deal out of wanting his vodka martini stirred rather than shaken. In his semi-inebriated state, it had made sense that ordering his drink prepared opposite of the way James Bond demanded them would make him seem unique and mysterious. Later, when he'd sobered up, he'd realized that caring so much about how the martini was mixed at all had simply marked him as an asshole. He was pretty sure he remembered a smirk on Frank's face when he'd ordered that first vodka martini.

There was no question about the smirk on Frank's face, tonight, however, as the man dropped two olives into the glass and set it in front of Jennings on a napkin. "To her Majesty's health, J.," he said in a fair impersonation of Sean Connery's Scottish brogue. His eyes widened in amusement.

Suddenly, Carl Jennings's entire life seemed no more than a ridiculous parody of all he'd ever wanted to be. Without looking up to meet the bartender's eyes he drained the glass, set it back down on the napkin and said, "Bring me another."

"Quite right, J.," the bartender rasped again. "*Stirred* of course, not—"

"Just shut the fuck up and bring the drink, Frank," Jennings blurted. "I don't give a damn *how* you mix it." He jerked slightly, surprising even himself at his own sudden aggression.

Frank froze for a second. His eyelids dropped in what Jennings could only interpret as regret, and he said, "I'm sorry, Carl. I didn't mean anything by—"

Jennings waved a hand in front of his face and shook his head. "I know," he said.

Frank took the glass and moved off to mix another martini.

Jennings glanced quickly around the bar to see if anyone else had witnessed the embarrassing incident. It didn't appear so. The place was beginning to fill up with the usual clientele—mostly low to midlevel Washington bureaucrats grateful for the end of another tedious day. He had come to the Shamrock alone this evening, wanting to be by himself. But he recognized a few other DHS employees at a table near the front door, and wondered if they, too, had become as disillusioned with their work as he had.

Maybe they hadn't, he thought, as Frank set the fresh drink in front of him and hurried away again. Maybe they had never wanted to be more than they were now. Chances were good that they'd taken the government tests and that the first opening was in Homeland Security. Jennings had learned there were far more federal employees who cared about insurance, retirement plans and job security than there were those who entered government work with a definite goal in mind. Most of them wouldn't care what department they worked for as long as the paychecks and other benefits kept rolling in.

Jennings looked across the tables, then along the booths against the wall. Beige trench coats—all identical to his own—hung from the hooks attached the seat backs between the tables. The males all wore gray or blue suits with subdued ties, and the women wore female equivalents of the sexless garb. Jennings had the ability to zero in on specific conversations—it was a talent he had perfected back in the days when he believed he'd someday be doing important intelligence work. As he listened, he heard accents from every region of the United States, and a few from Puerto Rico and the Philippines. But the words spoken were meaningless drivel, and he blocked them out again as quickly as he heard them.

The disgruntled DHS man was on his fourth martini when the door opened and a short, stocky man wearing a camel-hair overcoat and brown snap-brim hat walked in and moved directly to the other end of the bar. Jennings had seen him in the Shamrock several times before, always alone, always in the same hat and coat. Frank evidently remembered him, too, because without asking he turned to the bottles behind the bar and grabbed Pernod. Pouring a shot of the yellowish licorice-smelling fluid into a glass, he filled it the rest of the way with mineral water and took the cloudy-looking concoction to the man.

Jennings watched the man in the hat look down at the drink and nod to the bartender. While he didn't speak, Jennings had heard his voice before. He spoke excellent English, but the accent wasn't American. It had a hard, low, throaty sound that Jennings suspected marked him as originating in the Middle East.

Jennings finished his martini, then decided to order one more, settle the bill, then down it and go home. Maybe he'd pick up a bottle of vodka on the way. Or maybe he'd just go back to his tiny, overly priced one-bedroom apartment and sit in the ragged reclining chair and let the alcohol he'd already consumed wear off. Sometimes when he did that he didn't even bother to turn on the TV. He would sit for hours some nights, alternating between daydreams of espionage glory and the depression that set in when reality pulled him back to the knowledge that such days were never to be.

"One more and the bill," Jennings said the next time Frank passed within earshot. "And hey, man…I really am sorry."

The bartender shrugged. "No sweat," he said. "We all have a bad day now and then."

Frank had reached for the vodka bottle when the man in the camel-hair coat and hat said something Jennings didn't catch. Frank nodded his way, poured the vermouth on top of the vodka and dropped in two olives. "Guy at the end of the bar's picking up your tab," he said as he set down the fresh drink with one hand and grabbed Jennings's empty glass with the other.

The DHS man started to protest but before he could speak the stocky man had left his seat and moved onto the stool next to him.

The man smiled beneath the hat brim. "Do not worry," he said in the thick accent. "I am not gay."

Jennings turned to look at him. "I didn't think—"

The accent interrupted him again. "Of course you did," the man said, smiling. His face was cracked, wrinkled, as if it had spent many years in the sun. "I would have, too. It is rare in this country for one man to approach another as I have just approached you unless he is a homosexual." He paused a moment, lifted the smoky glass of Pernod and water to his lips, then added, "But I assure you, that is not the case. I seek only conversation to pass a lonely evening. I have seen you here by yourself before, and thought perhaps you might feel the same need."

Carl Jennings had tensed when the man first sat down. But there was something about the odd little fellow that made him relax. Perhaps it was the sincerity he heard in the voice. Or maybe it was just the verbal confirmation that the guy wasn't some queer on the make. Whatever it was, the Homeland Security employee held out his hand and said, "Carl Jennings."

The hand which shook it was hard, strong, callused, and firm. "Moshe Singer," said the man who still wore the snapbrim hat. "From Tel Aviv."

7

Sometimes, in the middle of battle, time loses all relevance. All movement slows, and seems to move across the vision like a slow-motion replay. Other times, the warrior engaged in a life-or-death struggle might even feel as if he has split into two separate entities: the brain and the body. The brain entity stands to the side, watching and analyzing the situation, and telling the body what to do. The body obeys the brain's commands with a mindless, robotlike efficiency. The warrior recognizes that one false move will bring about his death. The man focuses completely and categorically upon the immediate threat, forcing out anything, and everything, which might distract him from the most basic human instinct of all.

Survival.

Such was the case with the Executioner as he continued to sprint toward the man holding the Uzi behind the hat display. Time no longer had meaning, and while everything around him seemed to slow, his mind raced at a thousand times its normal rate as he considered every detail of the situation in which he now found himself. Potential actions rushed into his brain at the speed of light. Most were cast aside as just as quickly. A few were filed in the back of his mind for reconsideration a nanosecond later when he would make his final decision.

The Calico was jammed, there was no time to clear it, and neither the Beretta nor Desert Eagle could be reached before the man in the kaffiyeh pulled the Uzi's trigger. Bolan was too far away to lunge for the weapon, redirect the barrel and execute a disarm, and there was no suitable cover. If he dived right or left, the best he could hope for was that the al Qaeda killer's first rounds might miss him. And it would take only a fraction of a second for the terrorist to correct his aim.

If he went airborne, attempting to leap up and over the first burst of fire, the same thing would happen. The man behind the wall would need only to raise the Uzi's barrel a fraction of an inch to correct his aim, and Bolan would have bullets piercing his body long before he fell over the display rack onto the subgunner. He still had the vest, and many of the rounds would likely hit him there. But the al Qaeda man had already shot him in the chest three times; he knew about the vest— could even see it over the blacksuit now—and would aim for the head, or below the waist, or both with his sputtering automatic fire.

The options considered, the Executioner knew he had only one reasonable course of action. Only one option gave him even the slightest chance of living past the next few seconds.

Bolan hit the floor just below a 3-round burst. The rounds sailed an inch above his hairline as he landed on his left side in a semiseated position. As he slid along the tiles, his boots hit the Bass Pro Shop logo on the sheet hanging over the side of the display table as a second volley of fire exploded above him. Twisting at the waist, Bolan curled his legs under and threw his head forward. He slid through the sheet and under the table on his left shoulder and hip.

The Executioner felt a thigh strike the support beneath the folding table, and the leg snapped. A metallic screech sounded as one end of the display table fell. But by then he had slipped beyond the table along the tiles and had crashed headlong into the man behind it.

A rain storm of hats in every style and color fell over the Executioner and the man with the Uzi. The gunfire halted, and in the sudden silence Bolan heard the familiar wail of police sirens. There had been more than enough time since the gunfight began for the Springfield police to have been summoned.

The fact was, the Canadian Mounties or the Mexican *federales* had almost had time to arrive. But Bolan knew no law-enforcement officer was going to get there in time to help him.

Dropping the useless Calico, Bolan let the force of his slide carry him up to his knees. He could see that his impact had knocked the al Qaeda man onto his side. Like the Executioner's own submachine pistol, the Uzi had fallen to the floor. But the terrorist was reaching to retrieve the weapon and, as Bolan's hand shot toward the Beretta under his arm, the man's fingers closed around the grip.

A half step behind, Bolan knew there was no time to draw the Beretta. Leaning back, he grabbed the edge of the semi-collapsed table and used it to propel himself forward. Hats and caps flew through the air as he lunged toward the terrorist. At the same time, the al Qaeda man lifted the submachine gun and rolled onto his back, preparing to fire.

The Executioner came down on top of the man, his hands closing around the terrorist's wrists. He rode both arms down to the floor. A burst of fire shot harmlessly to the side, as Bolan landed astride his screaming adversary.

The Executioner pinned his opponent's arms to the ground over his head. He pushed downward as the al Qaeda man continued to scream and push upward. With both hands occupied, and in no position to use their feet, the two men strained against each other, each trying to overcome the other through brute force. The terrorist was strong. But Bolan knew he was stronger and, given time, he could wear the man down and disarm him.

But there was no sense wasting such time when there was a faster, easier way to end the conflict.

Suddenly releasing the pressure on the terrorist's arms, the Executioner dived down as his opponent's own strength—now freed from restraint—shot him up. Bolan aimed his head at the terrorist's chin, hoping to strike the tip. But at the last second, the al Qaeda man tucked his chin against his chest, and the Executioner's forehead struck the bridge of his nose instead. Bone cracked, and cartilage smashed with a sickening sound. Blood spurted from both of the man's nostrils.

Bolan closed his eyes and turned his head, avoiding the splatter. He had not knocked the man out as he'd hoped. But the terrorist was stunned, and for a moment he lay where he was, helpless. Pinning the Uzi to the ground again, the Executioner let loose of the killer's other wrist and shot his own hand behind his back.

The blade of the knife slid out of its sheath in an ice-pick grip. Before the terrorist could recover, Bolan had raised the knife high over his head. Seated as he was on the man's chest, the Executioner had no shot at the heart. But that mattered little.

Bolan brought the blade down with all the strength in his arm and shoulder. The thick, reinforced tip made contact just above the terrorist's left eyebrow and drove deeply into the skull. The Executioner twisted the blade within the man's brain, and the terrorist began convulsing spasmodically. Then he lay still.

Sirens could be heard all around the store, and through the windows the Executioner could see flashing red and blue lights. The place was surrounded by police, and if they found him, dressed in his blacksuit and Kevlar, they'd want to know who he was and why he was there. That would cause delays he couldn't afford. Not when more lives were at stake.

Quickly, the Executioner shook the dead al Qaeda man down and found exactly what he'd known he'd find—a money belt. He jammed it into a slit pocket of his blacksuit.

Standing up, the Executioner glanced at the jammed Calico on the other side of the splintered and warped plywood display wall. He no longer needed it, and it would just be in his way as he tried to make his way out of the building. Like the rifle he'd abandoned at the golf course, he'd let the police find it. Every detective in Springfield, and the entire state of Missouri for that matter, could spend the rest of their careers trying to trace the serial number on the weapon if they liked. The weapon would never lead them back to Stony Man Farm.

Bolan stooped and grabbed a brown corduroy hunting cap that had fallen from the display wall to the floor. As he stood back up, he heard a voice coming over a megaphone from somewhere on the upper floor: "This is the police! Drop all weapons and come out immediately and you will not be harmed!"

From somewhere close to the stairs on the lower floor he heard a rustle, then whispers. Had he missed one of the terrorists? He realized quickly that the voices he heard were those of people—employees, café customers, or maybe even Choate and Appleby—who had taken cover when the shooting started. Now that the shooting had stopped they were wondering whether it was safe to come out of hiding.

Bolan wondered about the mayor and senator. Where were they? Had they been harmed? He didn't think so. He had never been more than a step and a half behind the al Qaeda men as they had made their way through the store. If the two politicians had been killed, he'd know about it.

Retracing his path through the lower floor of the store, the Executioner returned to the hunting wear department. Hurrying to a row of green cargo pants hanging against the wall, he grabbed a pair three sizes too large and pulled them up and over his blacksuit and the Desert Eagle. Hiding the Kevlar vest would be all but impossible, so he jerked loose the Velcro straps and let it fall to the floor. A stack of T-shirts bearing the jumping fish logo he'd already seen went over his head and the Beretta. But the weapon still bulged suspiciously, so he slid his arm into a black-and-red plaid mackinaw. The corduroy cap, with earflaps tied up over the top, completed the disguise.

The voice on the megaphone returned to shout, "This is your last warning! Drop your weapons and come out now! If you do, you will not be hurt. If you do not, we cannot be responsible for your safety!" There was a pause, then the voice finished up with, "You have thirty seconds! Then we come in!"

The Executioner moved behind a circular rack of shirts and

dropped to one knee. He wasn't sure his outfit was going to fool anyone. But the disguise was the best he could come up with on such short notice.

He glanced to his watch.

Exactly thirty seconds after the voice on the megaphone had last spoken, he heard the sound of quiet footsteps moving on the floor above him. Unless he missed his guess, the first wave of the SWAT teams and whatever other cops would be searching the store should be right around the area where the cabin cruiser was suspended from the ceiling in the boating department.

He waited, hoping the searchers would find several innocent victims in hiding before they came to him. Let them get used to frightened bystanders, and he stood a better chance of slipping through their fingers himself. All he had to do was feign enough fear to pass as just another early morning customer caught in the wrong place at the wrong time. And hope they paid no attention to the overcoat that hid the Beretta.

It took nearly half an hour for the Springfield police to search the upper floor. Finally, Bolan heard the soft sounds of rubber-soled boots making their way tentatively down the steps. He parted the shirts in front of him quietly, peering through the dropping sleeves to see a half dozen men in full SWAT gear, including helmets with face shields, descend to the lower floor. The men carried the best possible weapons for such a job—MP-5 submachine guns. But their approach tactics could have used some work. Bolan couldn't help thinking that if he, or any other reasonably good marksman with an assault rifle or submachine gun, had wanted to, he could have taken out half of them on the stairs before they'd even reached the lower floor.

The Executioner watched a man with sergeant's stripes on the sleeves of his coveralls wave four of the men toward the camping section to the left of the steps. Four more moved out toward a sign marked Team Sports. The sergeant then led his remaining three men toward the section where Bolan was hidden.

The quartet divided again, and began walking the section row by row. Roughly halfway to the shirts behind which the Executioner knelt, he saw one of the SWAT men suddenly halt in his tracks. The folding stock against his shoulder, the man in blue aimed his MP-5 at something out of sight behind a shelf filled with jeans.

A moment later, the SWAT officer lowered his weapon and helped an elderly woman to her feet. He held a finger to his lips for silence, then took her arm and turned her around. Quickly, he unsnapped a leather pouch on his belt and produced three plastic flexible cuffs. Wrapping one around each of the woman's wrists, he connected them behind her back with the third.

The Executioner frowned. The old woman was as far from fitting the profile of a terrorist, or criminal of any kind, as they came. Which meant the cops planned to take everyone they found in the store into custody. They'd sort the "good" from the "bad" later.

Bolan watched through the shirts as the SWAT officer quickly frisked the woman. It was a quick, general pat-down designed not only to look for weapons but to keep from getting sued in case she later claimed he had groped her.

But the Executioner didn't try to fool himself. The SWAT man wouldn't be as worried about law suits when it came to a man like him. And he'd be far more concerned about the potential threat of a man Bolan's size than he was with a little old lady.

He'd find the Beretta and Desert Eagle—there was no doubt about that. Then he'd find the blacksuit underneath the hunting clothes, and the Justice Department credentials. All of which would add up to a lot of questions.

Bolan knew he would appear more suspicious than if he'd just stood up in his combat gear and flashed his badge when the police had arrived.

Bolan watched the SWAT man lead the weeping woman to the foot of the stairs, then hand her off to another man in black who escorted her to a third combat-geared cop. The third man took the woman out of sight toward the upper level.

Bolan changed his plans. He had no time now to doff the hunting wear over his blacksuit, so he left it in place and continued to wait. The outer clothing could still serve a purpose—just not the same one he'd originally thought it would.

The Executioner was still kneeling when the same cop who'd cuffed the woman suddenly stepped around the shirt rack, spotted him and swung the MP-5 his way. "Freeze!" the man ordered in a harsh whisper.

It was obvious that the cops were maintaining as much silence as possible under the circumstances. They didn't want to be in the process of arresting one person just to have another jump up two rows away and tear into them with automatic fire.

Bolan had already held up his hands passively when the order had come. Still kneeling, he said, "Is it over? Have you caught them?" He forced a worried look to cover his face.

The SWAT man didn't answer. And Bolan could not see

his face through the face shield attached to the front of his helmet. But he heard the next words as clearly as the first.

"Stand up."

Slowly, as if his knees were weak, the Executioner rose.

"Turn around."

Limping slightly to further his look of helplessness, Bolan turned his back to the officer.

The cop was cutting him no slack with procedure. But Bolan hoped believing his act, combined with the fact that the man had already found the old lady, had gone at least partway toward convincing the cop he'd stumbled onto another terrified victim rather than a terrorist.

Bolan wanted the man to lower his guard. At least until the cuffs were on and he started finding guns. Bolan figured he would be, at best, detained. At worst, if the cop was jumpy enough after all that had happened, Bolan might just get a volley of MP-5 fire in the back. The irony of having just thrown away his Kevlar vest wasn't lost on him.

Bolan waited. As soon as he heard the snap of the leather pouch he whirled around. His elbow caught the SWAT man in the jaw, and a handful of plastic cuffs dropped to the floor. But the cop was big, strong, and one elbow wasn't going to put him down for the count.

One of the Executioner's right crosses did, and the SWAT officer toppled to the floor.

Bolan made a fast 360-degree turn. In the distance, he could see the other members of the SWAT team moving cautiously through the rows of clothing and equipment. But the closest man was too far away to have seen what had just transpired.

Two minutes later, the SWAT man still lay unconscious on

the floor. But, instead of the navy blue coveralls, helmet, and face mask he wore only the regular patrolman's shirt and pants, which he'd had on underneath.

Bolan's mackinaw and cargo pants lay to his side.

The Executioner finished zipping up the coveralls and shrugged into the nylon equipment vest. Glancing at the plastic tag opposite the embroidered badge, he saw the name DAVIS printed in large block letters. Pockets in the front and on the sides held extra 30-round magazines for the MP-5. All in all, the SWAT gear was a tight fit over his blacksuit and pistols but if no one took a second look—and he planned to do nothing which would cause them to—he ought to be able to make it out of the building before the man on the floor woke up and sounded the alarm.

Grabbing the MP-5 off the floor, the Executioner flipped the face mask down over his eyes and started for the steps.

He was halfway there when one of the other SWAT men pushed a young man wearing plastic cuffs and a grease-stained apron out from between a tall row of backpacks. Seeing Bolan, he nodded, then whispered, "You going back up, Gary?"

The Executioner nodded behind the dark face mask.

"Take this guy, will you?" the man whispered again. "I've got another one hiding a few rows down." Then, turning his attention back to the frightened man in the apron, he added, "Claims he's a cook. Probably is. But you know what the sarge said."

Bolan nodded again. Reaching out, he grabbed the young man's arms and walked on toward the steps. At the bottom of the stairs, the SWAT man standing guard and starting the relay of prisoners toward the top floor said, "You taking him up yourself, Gary?"

The Executioner nodded for the third time, glad that he had been asked only yes or no questions. He pushed the cook ahead of him up the steps. He passed the SWAT team member stationed halfway up the flight without incident, then continued up the steps to the upper floor.

At the top, Bolan grabbed the young man's arm again and led him down the aisle, toward the front of the store. The terrified kid started to speak, but the Executioner growled "Keep your mouth shut" in a low, menacing voice. "We'll straighten it out in a minute."

The kid nodded and did as he was told.

Bolan walked toward the boating department. Just past the cabin cruiser hanging from the ceiling, he could see a dozen officers. Some were SWAT, others in patrol uniforms, and a few wore the plainclothes of detectives. They had corralled at least ten people in the large entryway in front of the café. Most of the civilians wore name tags, and looked as if they worked at the store. A few—like the woman he'd seen handcuffed earlier—had to have been eating breakfast when the shooting started.

There was no sign of Mayor Choate or Senator Appleby.

Pulling the kid in the apron, Bolan saw that the cops were speaking briefly with each handcuffed prisoner, satisfying themselves that they were innocent victims, then severing the plastic handcuffs with a wire cutter. As he walked under the hanging boat, the Executioner heard one of the plainclothes men speak to an acne-faced teenager.

"Go on in the café and take a seat," the detective said as he snipped the plastic behind the kid's back. "Someone will be in to take your statement as soon as the bottom floor's been cleared."

The teen nodded and rubbed his wrists as he practically ran into the café area.

When he reached the entryway, Bolan shoved the man in the apron toward the group still in cuffs and continued toward the door. But as he did, a uniformed officer wearing lieutenant's bars on his shoulders stared at him and frowned, then looked at the name tag on his coveralls. Staring even harder now at the face mask covering the Executioner, the man had opened his mouth to speak when a commotion behind them in the boating area suddenly drew all heads in that direction.

Bolan turned like the rest of the cops but kept walking toward the door. As he watched, he saw another of the SWAT officers making his way down the steps that led to the cabin cruiser.

Following behind him were two shaking, disheveled and red-faced men. One wore a cowboy hat at an awkward angle. The other had gray hair that looked as if it had just been through a tornado.

The Executioner shook his head. He finally knew where Mayor Choate and Senator Appleby had been. And that the only thing wounded had been their pride.

Bolan looked over the parking lot as he walked out the door. He could see the Maxima. It had been shot full of holes at the beginning of the gunfight. He doubted it would even start, let alone run. And even if it did, the bullet-riddled body would draw too much attention.

Bolan saw a black-and-white squad car standing in the middle of the drive between the parking spaces. The officers who had arrived in the vehicle had deserted it with the driver's side door still open. The engine was still running. It was almost as if they'd left it there for him. Besides, Bolan thought, the way he was dressed, no one would even notice him sliding behind the wheel.

Stopping quickly at the trashed Maxima, the Executioner popped the trunk and pulled out his suitcases and equipment bags.

A moment later, he was speeding away in the black-and-white, lights and siren heralding his departure.

TEN MILES AWAY from the Bass Pro Shop Bolan pulled off the interstate into another business area. He had killed the lights and siren shortly after leaving the scene of the gunfight. He decided to ditch the squad car behind a small strip mall. For a second, he considered discarding the SWAT gear. But as he was about to unzip the coveralls, a young mother and a boy around five years of age came out of the back entrance to a dress shop.

"Look, Tommy," the mother said, smiling at her son. "Another SWAT policeman!"

The boy smiled shyly, looking up at the Executioner. "My daddy's a policeman, too," he said. "He works SWAT."

Bolan smiled and squatted down next to the boy. "What's his name?" he said.

"Gary," the boy said.

"Gary Davis," the woman said, then frowned as she looked down at the Executioner's name tag. She had started to speak when the Executioner said, "Well, my name's Davis, too, Tommy. But my first name is John." Reaching out, he shook the kid's hand. "I've met your daddy. But we're not related. At least not that I know of."

The woman was still frowning as Bolan stood back up. "I thought I'd met everyone on the SWAT team," she said. "We had a barbeque a couple of weeks ago and—"

"I didn't come on until a couple of days ago," the Executioner said. He glanced at his watch. "Sorry, but I've got to run." He smiled again, this time at the mother. "It was nice to meet you both, and I hope I'll be invited to the next barbeque."

"Why, of course," Mrs. Davis beamed.

Bolan turned and walked quickly around the end of the shopping strip. It was, indeed, he decided, a small world. And while Springfield might have a population of well over a hundred thousand people it was still a small town. He was just happy that news of the SWAT call-out at the Bass Pro Shop hadn't caught up to Gary Davis's wife yet.

And that he'd stolen the uniform of an officer named Davis instead of "Viriyapah" or "Ziegelgruber."

Bolan hurried around to the front of the mall. Fifteen seconds after opening the door, he had smashed the steering column of another average-looking Nissan Maxima and started the engine.

Taking to the interstate once more, Bolan waited until he saw what looked like an industrial area ahead and took the next exit. Turning off onto a side street, he drove slowly until he found the right spot.

Pulling down an alley, Bolan killed the engine, pulled the key from the ignition, and grabbed the SWAT helmet and the MP-5 from the seat next to him. He popped the trunk, then exited the Maxima, walked swiftly to the trunk and opened it. A moment later, he had shed the SWAT gear and blacksuit and pulled on a pair of faded blue jeans, a white T-shirt, and

cross trainers. The Beretta was back under his left arm with
the extra 9 mm magazines balancing the shoulder rig under
his right. He slid the Concealex hip holster back onto his belt
and jammed the Desert Eagle into it, hearing the familiar
clicking sound as the weapon rammed home. A new knife was
placed at the small of his back with all three weapons covered by a brown, suedelike, microfiber jacket.

Just before he closed the trunk, the Executioner remembered the money belt he'd stuffed into his blacksuit. He pulled
it out and slammed the lid.

Back behind the wheel once more, Bolan unzipped the
belt. Inside he found cash, the keys to the Oldsmobile, what
was beginning to appear to be the standard al Qaeda issue Kel-
Tek .32 pistol, and a key card to a Super 8 motel room. There
was also a forged Missouri driver's license—a picture of the
last man the Executioner had killed had been glued over the
one on the plastic-laminated card, then more plastic had been
added on top.

Bolan shook his head. It shouldn't fool anyone. But held
up quickly, it had probably been enough for the quick scrutiny of the motel clerk at the Super 8.

Leaning back against the seat, the Executioner wished for
a moment that he'd been able to gather the money belts he
knew had to have been strapped around the other three terrorists at the Bass Pro Shop. But he'd had no time to search
them as he chased after the last man, and by the time he'd finished the police had had the bodies surrounded.

Bolan shook his head. There was no sense wasting time
wishing anything. The opportunity had been missed, that
was that, and there was no changing history. He stared at the

Super 8 key card he'd dropped on the seat next to him. With four men dead at the Pro Shop, the motel might well be a dead end. But he had to be sure.

8

Underestimating the enemy was the downfall of some of the greatest military leaders in history. But failing to recognize that the enemy was human—and therefore fallible—was just as big a mistake. Mack Bolan had seen the amateurish choice of sniper sites of the al Qaeda man at the Oak Lawn Country Club come close to turning the tide in his favor. The bottom line, he knew, was that terrorists were no different than any other form of criminal. Sometimes they were smart. But other times, they did things so stupid that cops, soldiers, and others were left scratching their heads at the stupidity of their decisions.

The terrorists Bolan sought hadn't been stupid. But they'd been lazy in covering their tracks.

Bolan stopped at the first Super 8 he passed on the highway, got a national directory for the chain and a city map of Springfield in the lobby and returned to the Maxima. By cross-referencing the two, he located the motel closest to the Bass Pro Shop, then pulled back onto the interstate. The attempted assassinations were no more earth-shattering than the sniper attempt—certainly not the big strike toward which the intelligence indicated al Qaeda was heading. But he had no better trail to follow so he would have to climb each rung of the ladder he was already on.

Fifteen minutes later, the Executioner was turning into the parking lot and parking under the archway in front of the motel lobby. He suspected he would meet resistance from the desk clerk. But the clock was running now. More al Qaeda attacks were planned—not only did Stony Man Farm know it from Kurtzman's scans of the internet and e-mail, Bolan could feel it. The bottom line was that he couldn't afford to spend time inserting the key card into every door of the motel like he had at the Sun View in Fredericksburg.

Swinging the glass door open, Bolan saw that the lobby area was deserted. He walked to the desk, waited a moment, then brought his hand down lightly on the round steel call bell on the countertop. A second later, through the open door that he assumed led back into the motel's office area, he heard the beeps and clicks of a computer. Then the creak of a metal desk chair—with wheels in dire need of oil—met his ears.

Bolan flashed his Justice ID. "I need to know which room Mr. Habbibi is in," he told the young clerk.

The young man looked uncertain. "We don't give out room numbers," he said. He stared hard at the Executioner, then relented. "I thought those guys were up to something though."

Bolan forced a friendly smile. "Your instincts are good," he said, flattering the young man. "It's a matter of national security," he said.

The desk clerk's eyes widened. He walked to the computer on the counter between them. He punched in a few buttons, and a moment later nodded at Bolan.

"Room 132," he said.

Bolan leaned toward the monitor and said, "There were four of them together. They'd all have names like Habbibi. Middle Eastern." He paused. "Find those other names and the room numbers for me, will you please?" he said.

"I don't have to look them up!" the youth said with a mixture of pride and excitement. "Rooms 132 and 134," he said. "Adjoining rooms."

"Thanks," Bolan said. "I've got a key to 132. But I'll need one for 134 in case the adjoining door's locked on the other side."

The young man gulped then nodded. He was obviously caught up in the drama of assisting a federal investigation. "I'll just get you the master key!" he said.

"Thanks again," Bolan said pleasantly. He took the card and stuffed it into his back pocket. "You've done your country a real service," he said.

The young man looked ready to burst with pride.

Bolan hurried through the lobby and out the door to the Maxima. Pulling it through the parking lot, he found the rooms he was looking for on the side of the building, ground floor. The master key let him into 132. The adjoining door to 134 stood open.

It took the Executioner even less time to search the rooms than he'd counted on. The rooms had been cleaned. They bore no trace of the terrorists who had slept there the night before.

Depression, or even negativity, had never been part of Bolan's psychological makeup. Such feelings were not only pointless, they were destructive, and he'd never allowed them to enter into his thought process. But the Executioner was far from happy as he closed the door to room 134 and returned to the Maxima. He had run up against another brick wall. And while he had no doubt that more al Qaeda strikes were in the works, he didn't have a clue as to what they were, or where they might be going down.

Driving out of the parking lot, Bolan pulled the cell phone from his pocket and tapped in the number to Stony Man Farm. Barbara Price picked it up on the first ring. "Hello, Striker," she said. "I was just about to call you. If you can believe the television, I'd say you had a busy morning."

Bolan drove down the access road along the highway, finally pulling into a convenience store and throwing the Maxima into park in front of the building. "Yeah," he said into the phone. "But it's led nowhere." He went on to report on his findings—or lack of them—at the Super 8 motel.

"Well," Price said as soon as he'd finished, "while you were running around, something else came up. You need to get for Edmond, Oklahoma," she said.

"What's in Edmond, Oklahoma?" Bolan asked.

"The University of Central Oklahoma. And a Liberal Arts building that has just been taken over by terrorists who claim to be al Qaeda," she said.

For a moment, the line went silent. Then Price added, "Jack's waiting for you at the airport."

Without another word, the Executioner backed out of the convenience store parking lot, pulled up the ramp to the interstate and headed back toward the airport where he'd arrived in Springfield a few hours earlier.

9

The fact that he was Jewish had never really been an issue in Carl Jennings's life. His parents had not been religious, and the name Jennings was about as bland as you got with Hebrew roots. He had never experienced any persecution, or even noted prejudices toward him as he grew up. Granted, once in a while one of his friends told a Jewish joke. But they also told Polish, English and French jokes, and none of them were ever mean-spirited—just funny.

So Carl Jennings was more than a little surprised at the sudden ethnic pride he had begun feeling after meeting Moshe Singer the night before. It was as if the man had awakened within him the first knowledge that he really did come from a people with a rich and colorful history. But Singer did not sugarcoat the truth, either.

"We have suffered tremendous persecution," the aging Israeli had said. "And we have meted out tremendous persecution ourselves."

That statement had stuck in Carl Jennings's inebriated brain the rest of the night, as well as entered his consciousness, off and on, the next day at work. By the time five o'clock rolled around, he was more than a little anxious to hurry back down to the Shamrock Tavern where he and Moshe Singer had agreed to meet again.

Jennings stirred his vodka martini with the swizzle stick and glanced at his watch. It was a little after six o'clock. The elderly Israeli was a few minutes late, and Jennings suddenly felt foolish. He had been watching the door as if waiting on his date to the high-school prom.

Around him were the regular weeknight Shamrock customers as well as a few unfamiliar faces. Frank was behind the bar again, and when he saw Jennings drain his glass he brought a second drink down to him. "On the house," the bartender said. "Sorry about the misunderstanding last night."

"Hey," Jennings said. "You don't have to do that." But he took the drink anyway. "No big deal. I was just in a bad mood."

"It's this town," Frank said, wiping the bar with a rag. "The longer you stay here, the more it crazy it makes you."

Jennings nodded at the man's back as Frank walked down the bar to where a man in one of the unofficial Washington, D.C., uniforms—the beige trench coat—had just taken a seat at the bar.

Five minutes later the door opened again. Moshe Singer walked in wearing the same camel-hair overcoat and snap-brim hat he'd had on every time Jennings had seen him. He unbuttoned the coat as he walked toward the Homeland Security man, a huge smile stretching out the lines of his weathered face. Stopping next to Jennings, he said, "Why don't we take a booth?" He nodded toward the only empty one left against the wall. "My back is hurting me tonight, and the thought of sitting on a stool makes it hurt even more."

Jennings smiled back at the man. He didn't know exactly

what it was about Singer that appealed to him. But even within the short length of time they'd known each other—less than twenty-four hours—he'd developed an affection for the older man. He followed the Israeli to the booth, and slid into the seat.

Moshe Singer took off his camel-hair overcoat and hung it on the hook outside the booth. The brown hat came off next and was hung over the coat.

Jennings was slightly surprised. Every time he had seen Singer, the man had kept both hat and coat on while he drank his Pernod and water. The young Homeland Security agent watched the Israeli lower himself painfully into the seat across from him. You learned something knew every day, he thought. Even creatures of habit sometimes changed those habits.

Singer placed both hands on the table in front of him, palms down, then arched his back and grimaced. A moment later, the older man smiled. "Ah," he said. "Much better."

"How did you hurt it?" Jennings asked.

"I fell off of a camel," Singer said with a straight face.

Jennings frowned, not sure what to make of the statement.

"It was a joke," Singer said. "Relax, my young friend. Did you not tell me you were Jewish yourself last night?"

Jennings nodded.

"Then laugh," Singer said. "If we Jews cannot laugh at ourselves, then who can we laugh at?"

Jennings cracked a smile. He wondered why it was he could laugh so hard at the ethnic-stereotype jokes his friends had told in high school, but found it so uncomfortable now when one was made about Jews, to a Jew, by a Jew.

"Do you know what your problem is?" Moshe Singer asked, a smile of irony on his face now.

Jennings grinned. "I've got so many, I don't know which one you're referring to," he said.

Singer laughed, a deep, throaty laugh. "The problem to which I refer," he said, "is the fact that until you met me last night you had never realized that you were Jewish."

The statement caught Jennings off guard. But as he thought back over his life, he realized it was true. He had been told by his parents that he was Jewish, but he had never really known it. The sudden realization flowed through him now like a warm stream. It gave him a sense of belonging; of being a part of something bigger than himself. It was a feeling he had hoped to get by serving his country through the Department of Homeland Security. But that feeling had never come.

Before he could answer again, Frank walked over with a tray. Setting a fresh martini down in front of Jennings, he laid two tall cloudy glasses of Pernod and water in front of Singer. "I figured you had a little catching up to do," the bartender said. "By the way, these are on the house, too."

Jennings started to protest, but Frank waved a hand in front of his face. "Don't worry—after this one, you pay. But I figured I owed you two at least a couple of free ones after entertaining me like you did last night." He chuckled as he dropped the empty tray down to his side. "Damn, I thought any minute you guys were gonna jump up and start singing the soundtrack to *Fiddler on the Roof.*"

Singer laughed again but Jennings felt his cheeks coloring. He had drunk far more than even he was accustomed to last night, and paid for it all day with a headache. Only now, with a new drink under his belt, was the throbbing beginning to go away. He remembered getting excited, and feeling more and more Jewish as Singer told stories about growing up in Israel. He could only guess at what kind of childish fool he had to have looked like to Frank.

The bartender walked away, and Jennings took a drink of his martini. He and Singer made small talk, chatting about the way Washington had changed over the years, and the almost total lack of Jewish identity in the city. The Israeli seemed to find Jennings's lack of racial awareness amusing rather than offensive.

Before he realized it Jennings had drained his third martini. As he set the glass back down, Frank suddenly appeared with another double round. "Happy hour," he said, smiling. "Two for the price of one. But now you pay."

Jennings was faster than his older friend and had his wallet out first. He handed the money to Frank, waving him away with a generous tip, then stuck the wallet back into his pocket.

The men talked on. "Tell me more about Israel, Moshe," Jennings said.

"I will be happy to tell you more about Israel, if you are not bored with the ramblings of an old man," he said. He looked toward the rear of the Shamrock. "But old men have old bladders. And first, I must drain mine." He stood up and started to shuffle off. Then, suddenly, he stopped and looked back toward his coat and hat on the hook outside the booth. Hesitating for a moment, he glanced at Jennings, then walked on toward the restroom in the rear.

Jennings finished another martini, wondering what the weird double take had been all about. Surely Singer didn't think he would steal his hat and coat, or pilfer his pockets for money? So why had he stared back at the hook? If theft had not been the old Israeli's concern, there were only two possible answers. First, there could be something in the pockets the old man didn't want anyone to see. The other possibility Jennings considered was that he was making a big deal out of nothing, that he was so bored and disillusioned with his job he was letting his imagination run away with him.

Jennings downed half of his fourth martini and realized that even if it was his imagination he should be thinking like that. There was always a chance that some day he'd be transferred to a division within Homeland Security where he actually could perform a little real live espionage for his country. And if he was going to be a spy some day, it wouldn't hurt to start thinking like one now. Nor would it hurt to start brushing up on his craft.

Setting the glass down on the table in front of him, Jennings glanced over his shoulder in time to see Singer shuffle through the door to the men's room. He turned back to the coat on the hook, suddenly aware that he had to look through it—even if only for the practice. He didn't know what he'd find that embarrassed the old man. Maybe pornography. Maybe some indication that Singer really was gay—denying it had been the first words out of the Israeli's mouth the night before, and now that seemed an odd way to start a conversation.

Or maybe Singer was carrying bundles of cash, or diamonds, or whatever. It didn't matter what he'd find inside the coat. Whatever it was, he'd leave it there. Jennings just knew he had to find it.

He glanced over his shoulder again, then down at his watch. Singer would just be getting to the urinal. And he remembered that the man had made several trips to the men's room the night before, and taken a long time on each one. Old men not only had old bladders they had old prostates, and it took them awhile to get started.

Jennings rose suddenly and impulsively from the booth, about to begin looking through the coat less than three feet from where he sat. Then the realization that he had no backup plan hit him, and he dropped back down in his seat. He needed a story—some legitimate *reason* to be pilfering through the old man's pockets in case he came out of the restroom and caught him. Lifting his martini glass, he took another drink, then found the answer in his empty glass as he set it back down on the table.

He had two empty martini glasses. His eyes shot across the table. One of Singer's drinks was almost empty. The other hadn't been touched. That was close enough. It was time to order more drinks while it was still Happy Hour. He had paid for the last round. He remembered the angle at which he'd held the wallet, and even if Singer had been watching Jennings knew he could not have seen the other bills inside. If the man came out while he was looking through the coat he would laugh in embarrassment and say he'd forgotten to get to the bank. He was looking for money to pay Frank for the next round of drinks.

Jennings felt a thrill run through his body as he realized there was another convincing aspect to such a story. Looking through another man's coat pockets while he was gone was like walking into someone's house without knocking. It showed the kind of familiarity that only a close friend would take for granted. It was perfect.

Jennings caught Frank's eye behind the bar and raised one of his empty glasses. Frank nodded but held up one finger as he mixed a cocktail for a man seated in front of him.

Jennings wasted no more time. Shooting to his feet, he turned toward the men's room, saw no sign of Singer emerging, and glanced quickly around the rest of the bar. All of the other patrons were busily engaged in conversations and paid him no mind. He jammed his fingers into the left side pocket of the camel-hair overcoat, and came out with a half-empty roll of Life Savers and a handful of pocket lint. The outer right hand pocket was empty. But when he opened the coat Jennings found a zippered pocket inside the left breast. Pulling the zipper back, he reached inside. His fingers brushed the top of a thin leather wallet, and after another quick scan to make sure no one was watching, he pulled it out quickly and opened it.

It wasn't a wallet. At least not one for carrying money. It was more the kind of leather case cops carried. There was no badge inside but an identity card with Singer's picture on it was on display through a sheet of clear plastic. The printing on the card was in Hebrew, a language Jennings couldn't read. But he didn't have to be able to read it to recognize one of the words at the top.

A flush of confusion came over Carl Jennings as he quickly dropped the credential case back into the coat and rezipped the pocket. He realized his hands were trembling as he took his seat again.

A moment later, Frank arrived with another pair of martinis and two more Pernods. With Singer still in the men's room there was no need for his cover story. He paid for the round. Frank left without comment, and Jennings felt himself wringing his hands.

The word on the ID card he had recognized was *Mossad*.

Moshe Singer was a Mossad agent. He was a member of the world-renowned Israeli intelligence agency.

Five minutes later, Singer shuffled back to the table and took his seat. Jennings concentrated hard, knowing he had to act as if nothing had changed. He had to keep the same expression on his face, speak in the same tone of voice; not do anything that would lead Singer to suspect he had discovered who the Israeli actually was.

But as soon as Singer sat down, he looked up and the smile on his wrinkled face slowly faded. He stared into Jennings's eyes, and the DHS man could tell immediately that Singer knew. Singer shook his head sadly back and forth. "You looked through my coat while I was gone," he said.

Jennings started to deny it. But he knew instinctively that would be senseless. So he just sat there with his mouth half-open, looking like half an idiot and feeling like a whole one.

After a long moment, Singer finally shrugged. "I guess the question now," he said, "is what do you plan to do with this information?"

10

The flight from Springfield to Oklahoma City was an up-and-down affair, with most of the hour it took spent with the Learjet rising to, then descending from, the altitude Jack Grimaldi had been assigned. He made radio contact, dipped a wing and prepared to set down on one of the runways at Wiley Post, just east of Will Rogers Airport. The unorthodox landing of the private craft at the airport usually reserved for cargo planes had been set up by Hal Brognola in order to save time. The big Fed had promised that a car would be waiting below, as well.

Bolan had changed into a gray suit, white shirt and conservative necktie during the flight. But the blacksuit—as well as other equipment—was packed in a small suitcase just behind his seat in the jet. At this point, he didn't know exactly what role he'd decide to take once he reached the university. It might be best to go clandestine. On the other hand, he might decide to take charge of the entire counterterrorism op himself. He'd make his decision after he arrived and got a feel for the situation.

The Executioner reached behind him and grabbed the suitcase as Grimaldi brought the plane to a halt at the end of the runway. Two vehicles were waiting on the tarmac as Bolan dropped down from the Learjet. One was a black-and-white squad car with the inscription *Oklahoma City Airport Police* on the door. The head and shoulders of a gray-and-blue uniformed police officer could be seen above the steering wheel.

The other car was a black Toyota Highlander. The Executioner walked toward the SUV. Another uniformed officer stood next to the driver's side of the Highlander. "You're Cooper?" he asked as Bolan approached. In his left hand, he held a key ring.

Bolan nodded, producing the Justice Department credentials that identified him as Special Agent Matthew Cooper. The cop glanced at the picture, then handed him the keys. "Good luck, Agent Cooper," he said. "From all I've been hearing over the scanner, you're gonna need it."

The Executioner tossed his suitcase into the back seat, and slid behind the wheel of the Toyota as the cop strolled back to the squad car. A moment later, the police vehicle drove away.

Bolan stuck the key in the ignition, fired the Highlander to life and put the transmission in drive. Cutting across the tarmac, he crossed a parking area, passed a row of cargo storage areas, and pulled out onto the road.

As Bolan approached the edge of the campus, he knew he was where he was supposed to be. But he hardly needed any street signs to tell him.

A hundred yards to his left, it looked like the circus had come to town.

The lawns, gardens, and parking lots around the two-story Liberal Arts building had been cordoned off with yellow tape and sawhorses. Running between dozens of police cars were cops dressed in every conceivable type of law-enforcement uniform. Several of the distinctive hats worn by the Oklahoma Highway Patrol were visible, as were plainclothesmen and -women wearing blue windbreakers that read *POLICE*. As he turned and drove toward the edge of the activity, Bolan could make out the specific emblem of the Edmond PD on several of the vehicles. But in addition to Edmond, there were cruisers from Oklahoma City, War Acres, Bethany, the Oklahoma County Sheriff's Department, and others.

One of the brown-uniformed highway patrolmen held up a hand as the Executioner came to a stop in front of the orange cones. He leaned down as Bolan held up his Justice Department ID, then waved him through. The Executioner pulled into the nearest parking lot, killed the engine and got out. He grabbed the arm of a cop who came jogging past. "Where's the command post set up?" he asked.

The cop nodded toward a long tractor-trailer truck in the middle of the next lot over, nearest the Liberal Arts building.

Bolan looked that way and saw telephone and electrical lines running in and out of the open rear of the trailer, connecting to a portable generator parked just to the side. "I'm heading there now," the cop said. "I'll show you."

The Executioner followed the man to the trailer, then up three wooden steps and through the open back doors. Inside, he saw what amounted to a moveable command center. Desks were bolted to the floor along the sides of the trailer, and through a screen at the far end Bolan could see a gun rack holding AR-15 rifles and 12-gauge shotguns. Several men, and two women, were busy on phones at the desks. Other men, wearing navy blue or black combat fatigues, jumpsuits, and other SWAT gear, stood at the ready.

Bolan had his credentials out again as his feet hit the top of the steps. "Who's in charge?" he asked a short-haired blond woman seated at the nearest desk.

The woman had her phone to one ear. Nodding over her other shoulder, she said, "OSBI Director Lawford just got here," she said. "He's in the back."

The Executioner weaved his way through the crowd toward the back of the trailer. At the final desk on the right-hand side, he saw OSBI Director Wayne Lawford.

Lawford looked up as Bolan approached. For a second the director frowned, wondering who the stranger was. "Cooper?" he said.

"Mr. Director," Bolan smiled. He'd heard the broad-shouldered man was a good and tough leader. Lawford had enough confidence to listen to other men's ideas, and he wasn't afraid to bend the law a little when that's what it took to get justice. He and Bolan were cut from the same cloth in much of their philosophy, which would make the Executioner's role—whatever that role turned out to be—much easier as events continued to unfold.

Lawford shooed another man in a suit out of the chair next to his desk, and Bolan sat down. "Run it down for me," the Executioner said.

"They could have infiltrated the building any time this morning," Lawford said. "The doors open at seven a.m., and any time after that they could have just walked in like students."

Bolan nodded, waiting for him to go on.

"We assume they began the takeover at shortly before 2 p.m. Students outside the building reported shots fired at that time, anyway. Their first call was logged in by the University Police at 1:57 p.m."

"The campus cops?" Bolan frowned.

"That's who they called." Lawford shrugged. "But we can rely on their information—they're good—not just door-shakers. Their chief's an old buddy of mine, and he's whipped them into as professional a department as you'll find anywhere these days."

"That wasn't what I meant," the Executioner said. "Usually the first call is to a news station."

Lawford shrugged his big shoulders again. "They knew it wouldn't take long for UCO to notify everybody else," he said.

"Weapons?" Bolan asked.

"We've had spotters in the taller buildings around campus for the past hour," Lawford growled. "They've seen a couple of Uzis and AK-47s through the windows. But for the most part, they're keeping away from the windows."

"How many hostages?" the Executioner asked.

Lawford shook his head. "That's impossible to know, too." He lifted a computer printout from the top of the desk and looked down at it. "If every kid who's enrolled in classes was in there, then the answer is 567. But these are college kids, remember. Gotta figure a good many of them have skipped. My estimate would be around four hundred."

The Executioner nodded. "Any demands yet?"

Again, Lawford's head shook. "Nope. Haven't heard anything from them since that first call to the campus boys. But they've told us to be waiting for another call at four o'clock. They'll tell us what they want eventually."

Bolan knew that the al Qaeda training video he'd watched

in Brognola's office was destined to be reproduced, with copies going out to various federal, state and local law-enforcement agencies. But he doubted OSBI had received their copy yet. "You know what they really want, no matter what they say, don't you?" the Executioner asked.

"To get their mugs on TV, then kill everybody inside and blow up the building," Lawford said. "They're al Qaeda, after all. It's what they do." The director didn't need any video to see the writing on the wall. He pointed toward a quickly installed land line on the desk. "Still, we've got to play the game for a while. We're keeping that number—linked into the university cops—open for them."

Suddenly, the breast pocket of the director's jacket began to buzz. He reached in, pulled out a small cellular phone and said, "Yeah?" A second later he added, "Honey, you know I can't talk to you right now. I'll call you—" He stopped in mid-sentence and listened again. Then, without speaking further, he punched the button to end the call and dropped his eyes to the floor of the mobile command center.

Bolan looked on curiously. It was odd behavior. The OSBI director was known to be the consummate pro, compartmentalizing things, and never letting anyone see him sweat. But he looked like he'd just been diagnosed with a terminal disease.

After several seconds had gone by, and the man had not moved, Bolan broke the silence by saying, "Lawford? You okay?"

Finally, the OSBI leader looked back up, and when he did he looked as if he'd aged twenty years. The Executioner could see that the whites of his eyes had turned pink, and the sockets themselves seemed to have darkened.

"No," Lawford said, finally looking Bolan in the eye again. "I'm not all right at all." His hand rose to the bridge of his nose. He squeezed it, and shut his eyes tightly. The man looked as if he was trying hard not to cry.

Lawford looked back down to the floor. "That fact is," he said, "I'm about as far from being all right as a man could be. That was my wife. My granddaughter's a student here at UCO. And she's inside that building."

11

The Executioner looked down at his watch. It was just before 3 p.m. They had slightly over an hour before the call came from the al Qaeda men inside the building. Then, they'd hear a long and unreasonable list of demands that not even the terrorists themselves expected to be met. It would all be for show. For publicity. For airtime.

Unless Bolan could change things, no one was leaving the UCO Liberal Arts building alive.

In the corner of his eye, the Executioner saw a dark figure pushing his way toward the back of the command post trailer. He looked up to see a tall, athletic looking man in gold wire-rimmed glasses and a thousand-dollar navy blue suit. He'd taken off the jacket and had it slung over his shoulder, which revealed a badge clipped to his belt in front of a .45 Glock 21. He also wore a very fashionable pair of leather suspenders that were buttoned to his slacks, and shoes that looked like they'd cost more than the tractor-trailer in which the mobile command center had been set up.

All in all, Bolan thought, he looked more like an attorney than a cop.

Lawford looked up from the floor, saw the man and sighed. "Matt Cooper, meet Jack Recter. Cooper's Justice Department. Jack's the Special Agent in charge of the FBI's Oklahoma City office."

Recter ignored Bolan and spoke directly to Lawford. "I've coordinated the teams from the different agencies," he said bluntly. "The sooner we move out the better." He cleared his throat, for the first time glancing at Bolan as if offended that anyone else was with the OSBI director. "The closer it gets to 4 p.m., the more on guard they'll be."

"Just hold your horses a minute, Jack," Lawford said.

"Lawford, we can't—"

"You're obviously unfamiliar with the term 'hold your horses,'" the OSBI man said in a calm, controlled voice that was somehow full of menace. "So try 'shut the fuck up' on for size." He paused to let his words sink in, and watched the face behind the wire-rimmed glasses turn red.

Lawford turned to Bolan. "You were sent here for a reason," he said. "You have something in mind?"

Bolan glanced at his watch again. "Before we do anything else," he said, "we need to know exactly what's going on inside, where the hostages are, how many terrorists we're facing, everything."

"Well," Recter said sarcastically, "maybe we could send them a questionnaire to fill out. 'I'm sure they'd be happy to—"

"I said shut up, Recter!" Lawford boomed suddenly.

"I'm FBI, Lawford," Recter shot back.

"Which translates to 'Full of Bullshit and Ignorance' as far as I'm concerned," the OSBI director said.

The man in the expensive suit quit talking. His mouth

opened in shock. He obviously wasn't used to being spoken to in that manner, and it stunned him.

"My granddaughter's inside that building, Recter," Lawford said, taking a step toward the FBI man with both hands curled into fists. "And I'm not in any mood to put up with any of your ego today."

Bolan could see that the frustration Lawford felt was about to be taken out on the FBI agent. "Let's all settle down and see what we can work out," he said calmly.

The OSBI director turned toward him. "Okay," he said. "That's the first thing I've heard so far that makes sense." He took a deep breath and his fists straightened back into fingers. "Where the hostages are located. How many terrorists. All those things you mentioned—how are we going to find out about them?"

"Simple," Bolan stated flatly. "I'm going in."

Recter had recovered from his shock and now snorted through his nose. But another hard stare from Lawford kept him from speaking.

"Just how do you plan to pull that off?" Lawford asked. "These terrorists are Arabs, Cooper. You're dark. But not *that* dark. And the spotters tell us they're dressed like college kids and professors. You won't be able to hide that All-American mug of yours under a burnoose or kaffiyeh or whatever the hell those things are."

Bolan nodded. "No, there's no way I'm going to pass for one of them," he said. "So I don't intend to try."

"Then how—"

"By looking like a hostage," Bolan said.

The chatter in the rest of the trailer continued but Recter

and Lawford went silent for a moment. The OSBI director finally broke that silence by saying, "You want to commit suicide, why don't you shoot yourself in the head right now and save the trouble?"

"It's *worth* the trouble," Bolan said, "if I can save even one of the kids inside."

Turning to Recter, he said, "You want to make yourself useful, go find the field house."

"I don't work for Justice, Cooper, which means I don't take orders from you," Recter said, practically spitting.

"You do if you want to stay on-site," Lawford told him flatly. "You aren't in charge. I am."

"That's only until—" Recter started to say. He stopped halfway through the sentence when Lawford whirled toward him again and drew back a fist. Bolan reached and gently pulled the director's arm back down to his side.

Lawford relaxed. "What do you need from the field house?" he asked Bolan.

The Executioner looked at Recter as he answered. "Go to the football coach's offices," he said. "Get me a coaching shirt, a pair of slacks, shoes, everything. Tell the coach I want whatever they'd wear on an average practice day, like today."

Recter stared daggers through the man giving him his orders. "What sizes?" he asked sarcastically.

Bolan told him.

The FBI agent looked back to Lawford, who waved his hand and said, "You heard the man."

Recter slid his arms into his jacket, buttoned the middle button, adjusted his cuffs, then walked out with all the dignity he had left.

"Royal pain in the ass, that man," Lawford said, following Recter out with his eyes.

"He trying to take over?" the Executioner asked.

"Yeah, but this is state property. I've still got jurisdiction until this is officially declared an incident of international terrorism." Lawford sighed. "With any luck, maybe we can get it over with before he and the other Feds move in and screw it up." He remembered who he was talking to and added, "Present company excepted, of course. I trust Brognola and he trusts you." He sat back down and looked over at Bolan. "Thanks for calming me down.

"Don't mention it."

Lawford sat forward in his chair, all business again. "Okay," he said. "I've heard you can do the impossible, Cooper. But you really are taking your life in your hands."

"No, I'm taking your granddaughter's life, and the life of a bunch of other people's grandchildren, in my hands," Bolan replied.

Lawford nodded grimly. "So how do you plan to get in? They'll have all of the doors and windows covered."

"You had any surveillance of the roof?"

"Helicopters have flown over periodically. There's no sign of anyone up there."

"Good." Bolan nodded. "I want one of those helicopters to drop me in."

Lawford shook his head. "Chopper gets down that close, they'll hear it."

"Not if there's enough other noise," Bolan said. "There's an Air Force base in one of the suburbs here. Tinker?"

Lawford nodded. "Right, Tinker. In Midwest City."

"I'll need some jets to fly over low. We'll time the chopper drop with them." Bolan looked at the man, wondering what kind of hell he had to be going through, knowing his granddaughter was held hostage by insanely radical men bent not only on her destruction but their own. "And we'll have to do the same thing at a prearranged time to get me out of there. If you can't arrange it with the Air Force, I can."

"You've got enough on your plate as it is," the OSBI director said, lifting his cell phone. "Besides, I know the wing commander."

"One more thing," Bolan said as Lawford tapped numbers into the phone.

The OSBI man raised his eyebrows.

"I want my own pilot flying the chopper," he said.

Lawford made the call to the Air Force base, then called another number and ordered the helicopter. When he hung up this time he set the cell phone back on the desk. "OCPD chopper will set down on the football field," he said. "Two blocks that way." He pointed out the back of the trailer. "Your man will be flying it, and he'll have radio contact with the jets from Tinker."

"Good." Bolan looked down at the desk next to the man and saw a set of architectural drawings of the Liberal Arts building. The top page showed the ground floor. Just inside the door, on both sides of the main entrance, which faced the parking lot where the command center had been set up, were office suites. Between the suites was a wide hallway that included vending machines, tables and chairs. Two halls ran down the sides of the building with classrooms on both sides. The only deviation was on the east side of the building, where a large area marked Pegasus Theater took the place of several classrooms. Simple enough.

The Executioner rolled the large page to the side and looked down at the layout of the second floor. Other than the fact that there was no theater, and a stairway on the west side of the building led up to the roof, the second story was identical.

Bolan frowned at the page. He'd have to descend those stairs to get inside. And while the terrorists might not have anyone stationed on the roof itself, the enemy was bound to have the door to the stairs covered inside. But he knew it was still his best bet.

Bolan had seen the Liberal Arts building itself upon his arrival. It was a pragmatic, no-nonsense structure with none of the Ivy League bent he'd seen on other, older buildings as he'd driven onto the campus. It meant he'd be rapelling onto a flat roof rather than trying to keep from being impaled on a steeple.

Bolan turned to Lawford. "Any of the campus police around?" he asked.

Lawford nodded and picked up his cell phone again. "Theodore still out there?" he asked someone. A second later, he said, "Ask him to come in."

A moment later, a man wearing tan uniform pants and a darker brown shirt came threading his way to the rear of the trailer. The belt around his waist carried a .357 Magnum Smith & Wesson Model 66, and the gray steel of the gun was a perfect match for his hair. Also on the belt were two speed-loader cases, a handcuff case and an old-fashioned 12-loop cartridge carrier. The man's jaw was firm, and he had the hardened look of a cop who'd come up through the ranks through hard work rather than knowing the right people. He stopped in front of the desk and stared down at Lawford and Bolan.

"Cooper," Lawford said, "meet UCO Chief Jonesy Theodore. We were on an undercover task force together years ago when we were still young and full of spunk. Since then Theo has been on every police and sheriff's department in the state at one time or another."

The UCO chief laughed. "Well," he said, "maybe not *every* one."

"Theo, this is Matt Cooper," Lawford continued. "Justice Department."

Theodore reached out and shook the Executioner's hand with hard callused fingers. "Tell me something, Theo," Bolan said. "The doors to the classrooms—they have windows in them?"

Theodore nodded. "Small rectangular ones. Just above the doorknobs." He anticipated Bolan's reason for asking and said, "A man who stayed low could look in without being seen. Unless they happen to be looking directly at the door."

"What departments are inside?" Bolan asked.

"English and Creative Studies—that's the writing program. Humanities, Criminal Justice and—"

"Criminal Justice?" Bolan asked, interrupting. "You mean there may be *cops* in there as hostages?"

Theodore shrugged. "Maybe some," he said. "But what you'll have this time of day are primarily kids who plan to be cops when they graduate. Most of the working officers hit the building for night classes."

"But there might be a few who work the night shifts," Lawford said, and it was obvious he had not known the Criminal Justice department was in the building. "If there are, and the al Qaeda men searched them—"

"Which they *will* have—" Theodore said.

"Then they're already dead," Bolan finished.

Chief Theodore might not have seen the al Qaeda training video either, but he was nobody's fool any more than Lawford was. "I figure they were those first few shots the students outside reported," he said. "The terrorists would have reconned the place and known what departments were inside. They probably took out anyone with a gun or a badge first thing."

Lawford and Bolan sat silently. The situation had been personal from the start with innocent college kids and Lawford's granddaughter being threatened. Now, with cops being killed, it had grown even more personal.

Bolan shook his head. "Anybody at all who might be able to help from the inside?"

Lawford shook his head, too. "I don't know who would—" He cut himself off suddenly and said, "Wait a minute." Reaching back to his desk, he lifted the list of classes and students again and studied it.

"What?" Bolan asked.

"Professor Gary Williams," Lawford said. "He had an intro to novel writing class at 1:40."

"I know him," Theodore said. "He goes to the firing range with us sometimes and outshoots all my officers. Used to be one of yours."

Lawford nodded. "He did." He turned to Bolan. "Williams used to be an OSBI agent."

The Executioner's interest picked up. "Good one?" he asked.

Lawford smiled, the first time the Executioner had seen any trace of humor on the director's face since he'd arrived. "Depends on who you ask." He chuckled.

"Meaning?" Bolan prompted.

"Meaning he's an independent cuss," Lawford said. "Never took orders worth a damn. One of those guys who'd disappear and not report in for days. Then, just about the time you had enough to fire him, he'd show up with some major case solved." Now the OSBI director's chuckle became a full-blown laugh, and it was obvious a few memories of Williams were flooding through his brain. "Williams made it clear to one and all that he only followed men he respected. And he didn't suffer fools worth a damn—absolutely hated supervisors who'd snuck up the back ladder instead of doing their time on the street."

"How'd he end up as a professor?" Bolan asked.

"Sold a novel he'd written and didn't let the door hit him in the ass. The university hired him as an adjunct. He only teaches one or two classes a semester. Still writing."

The Executioner frowned. "Is he going to be an asset or a liability?" Bolan asked. "Assuming he's still alive?"

"Oh, he'll go down swinging for you," Lawford said. Bolan saw Theodore nodding affirmation. "Always had to be the first inside when there was a door to be kicked. And he'll just *love* anybody crazy enough to do what you're about to do."

"Will he be armed?" Bolan asked.

"Armed professors violate university policy as well as state law," Lawford said, "so I'd say probably so." His voice had an ironic tone to it that wasn't lost on the Executioner.

UCO Chief Theodore laughed. "Like I said, Cooper, I know him, too. I think I can give you a pretty definitive yes. He'll at least have a hideout gun someplace on him."

"Well, let's hope they didn't find it and kill him, too," Bolan said. "What classroom does he have?"

Lawford looked back to his list. "It's 119," the director said. "Downstairs, east hall."

The Executioner nodded, filing it all away for future reference. If Williams was armed, and if the terrorists hadn't found his weapon, and if he hadn't lost his cool and been killed already for some other reason—which sounded like it might be a real possibility with a guy like him—then maybe he'd be of some use when Bolan got inside.

But there were an awful lot of ifs at work. All Bolan could hope for was that the terrorists wouldn't search an English professor as thoroughly as they did Criminal Justice types.

The bottom line, the Executioner knew, was that he couldn't count on help from anyone—cops, ex-OSBI agents, or anyone else—once he'd entered the building. As usual, he'd be on his own.

Bolan looked up from the desk just as Recter reappeared carrying a blue-and-gold gym bag. The expression on the FBI man's face hadn't improved, but he'd learned to keep his mouth shut. He dropped the bag on top of the desk without a word.

Bolan quickly changed into the coaching uniform, leaving his suit, the Desert Eagle, Beretta and knife folded on top of Lawford's desk.

"You're going in *unarmed?*" the OSBI director asked incredulously.

"I don't see that I have any choice," Bolan said. "I'll stay out of sight if I can. But I'd say there's about a ninety percent chance that I'll be spotted before I've reconned the whole building. When I am, I'll be searched."

"They'll take you hostage, too," Recter said, and he sounded as if the idea held a certain appeal for him.

"Maybe," Bolan said. "Maybe not. We'll see."

"You're crazy," Recter said.

Bolan tied the laces on his athletic shoes. While the other three men had been talking, Theodore had bent over and pulled a pant leg up. Now he produced a 2-shot Davis .32-caliber derringer from his boot and said, "Here. Take this."

Bolan shook his head. "Thanks," he said. "But no thanks. If I was going to take that, I might as well take an M-60. Besides, if I need a gun there'll be plenty inside."

The cell phone on top of the desk rang shrilly. Lawford jerked it into his hand. "What?" he said. He listened for a second, then pressed the button to end the call and said, "Helicopter's ready. Recter, get someone to take Cooper to the field in an unmarked car." Standing up, Lawford stepped around Bolan and opened the screen door at the very end of the trailer. Just past the rifle rack the Executioner had seen upon entering, a trench coat hung from a hook in the trailer wall. Lawford snatched the garment off the hook and tossed it to Bolan. "They'll be watching from the windows, Coach," he said. "We don't want to burn you before you even get inside."

Bolan slid into the coat. Without another word he followed Recter out of the trailer.

THE PLANES OVERHEAD were so loud Bolan wished he'd worn earplugs. It took less than ten seconds for him to rapel from the chopper, and his athletic shoes hit the tar roof silently beneath the other noise. As soon as he'd landed, he unsnapped the harness, gave it a tug and watched Grimaldi dart the Oklahoma City police chopper up and away.

He moved swiftly to the steel door leading into the Liberal

Arts building. Chief Theodore had assured him that both this door, and the one at the bottom of the steps that opened into the second floor, would be unlocked at this time of day. But he'd provided a set of keys just in case. Bolan reached for the doorknob. He was unarmed, and for all he knew a madman stood on the other side, armed with a submachine gun or assault rifle. But if he intended to enter the building, he would have to find out.

There was no safer entrance, and the lives of approximately four hundred college students—one of them Wayne Lawford's own granddaughter—hung in the balance.

Bolan opened the door slowly, grimacing as the unoiled hinges screeched. The planes would have made the al Qaeda men nervous, at the very least. But the terrorists would know about the U.S. Air Force base located in the OKC metro area. With any luck, when no immediate assault followed the noise, they'd chalk it up to regular flight patterns.

The stairway was dark, but sunlight shot in as the door cracked open. Bolan held his breath. If he was going to get shot, now was when it would happen. He was almost surprised as he slid through the narrow opening, saw no one in the semilit stairwell, then closed the door behind him.

Descending the steps, the Executioner came to the second steel door. With no one on the roof or in the stairwell, he knew there had to be at least one man guarding the door on the inside. He planned to keep as low a profile as possible during this recon mission, avoiding the terrorists rather than killing them. But anyone he did encounter would have to be dealt with. And his instincts told him he was about to confront the first of such men.

The Executioner opened the door.

Immediately, the barrel of an AK-47 was jammed toward his face.

Bolan reached out, grabbing the hand around the rifle grip and sliding his other arm over and around the weapon. With a quick dip, then rise of his shoulder, he jerked the gun out of the terrorist's hands. As it came away, the snap of the man's elbow breaking echoed into the stairwell.

Only then did the terrorist's features come into focus. He wore a full beard and had dark eyes. The quick disarm, and the broken bone, had temporarily shocked him. But now the thin lips, all but hidden behind the thick black facial hair, opened wide to scream.

Bolan brought the stock of the AK-47 around in an arc, striking the man in the face. The crack of more bones breaking in the man's cheek echoed up the stairwell, and a pair of teeth fell from his open mouth. The Executioner reached out, grabbing the man by the hair and turning him 180 degrees. Slipping the rifle around his throat, he grasped the barrel in one hand, the stock in the other, and pulled his prisoner back into the stairwell.

The door to the second floor swung shut.

Bolan tugged the stock and barrel of the rifle with both arms. He felt the al Qaeda man's Adam's apple crush beneath the weapon. He increased the pressure against the throat until the flailing arms in front of him went limp.

He dumped the body in the corner of the stairwell, cracked the door open and looked into the hall. Deserted. He had been lucky for once—only one man had been stationed to guard the roof. Had there been two or more, particularly if they'd been spaced widely, he'd never have pulled it off.

He knew he couldn't count on luck like that more than once.

Closing the steel door again, Bolan looked down at the AK-47 in his hand. He was tempted to take it with him. But if he did that, and was spotted, it would ruin his whole football coach disguise. And if he didn't get spotted, he wouldn't need the rifle. For the recon mission he had planned, a weapon of any kind—other than his hands and feet—was more liability than asset.

Dropping the magazine from the AK-47, the Executioner cleared the chamber, leaned the barrel over the bottom step of the stairs, then jumped up into the air. Both athletic shoes came down in the center of the rifle, and the wooden stock broke away from the action and barrel, the crunch reverberating in the close confines of the stairwell.

The Executioner crept out from the stairwell, stepping around the doorway and looking down the hall to his left. An eerie silence hung in the air, and as the blueprints had indicated, he saw classroom doors on both sides of the hall. He'd have to check them all. But first, there were the office suites to his right. Walking lightly, he left the tiled hallway and stepped through a door onto a short-napped carpet. A black sign on the wall read *Humanities,* and below the word, in white letters, was a list of professors. A reception area with a desk, computer, several chairs and a small couch stood just inside the door. The area was empty.

As were the dozen or so smaller offices Bolan came to as he wandered through the suite, hoping to look like a football coach if any of the terrorists spotted him. His story would be that he'd been in the restroom when the takeover took place, and hidden there until he thought there might be a chance of escape. It was thin. Maybe so thin it would get him killed. But it was the best he could come up with under the circumstances.

While the offices Bolan searched were empty, there were signs that people had been there that day—and had left hurriedly. Several chairs had been turned over, and papers littered the floor. On the wall next to one desk he spotted several small drops of drying blood.

The same unsettling stillness he had encountered earlier still hung in the air as the Executioner retraced his steps out of the offices. Walking slowly, silently, his battle senses on high alert, he crept out onto the tiled hallway once more. Ahead, he could see that some of the classroom doors were open, others closed. He suspected the open doors meant empty rooms. But he couldn't be sure.

And he needed to know.

ALL OF THE ROOMS were empty. Some had showed signs of earlier occupation and a fast departure, while others looked as if they'd been empty all day. Bolan was surprised that no terrorists were patrolling the hallways. The only al Qaeda man he'd encountered had been the lone sentry covering the door to the roof. It didn't make sense.

Bolan wondered exactly how many terrorists were inside the building. It wouldn't take a lot of men with automatic weapons to hold terrified college kids at bay. But once the counterattack began, the fewer there were, the faster they could be killed and the longer it would take them to kill all the hostages.

Unless, of course, they had a bomb set up and ready. Then it wouldn't really matter how many of them there were. They were ready to die themselves, and the flip of a switch or a code punched into a remote-control device was all it would take.

A men's restroom stood at the corner of the building, and Bolan pushed his way in, checked each stall, then turned back and started to open the door again. As his hand grasped the vertical steel opening bar, however, he heard footsteps in the hall. He froze. A moment later he heard voices as the footsteps neared. Two men were speaking Arabic.

Moving away from the door, the Executioner waited for the footsteps to pass. They didn't. Instead, they halted briefly outside the men's-room door, and a moment later the door began to swing open. Bolan had no choice but to step back behind the door against the wall. And wait.

A tall man wearing a hooded gray University of Central Oklahoma sweatshirt entered the restroom. Baggy khaki cargo pants hung from the skinny hips below the sweatshirt, and on his feet were expensive Nike cross trainers. All of which looked somewhat incongruous with the 9 mm Uzi slung over his shoulder.

The Executioner saw the man catch sight of him in his peripheral vision. He had started to turn just as Bolan launched a right cross to the jaw. The punch connected, but some of the force was lost as the terrorist's head jerked to the side. The Executioner's fist still found his chin, however, and drove the man to his knees.

The second al Qaeda man was on his way into the restroom but was still half-hidden behind the door. Bolan reached out, grabbed the door and pulled it toward him. Then, using both hands, he slammed the door forward again.

The sound he heard was not unlike a baseball bat meeting a fastball.

The first terrorist was still kneeling on the floor, stunned. Bolan stepped back and brought a hammer fist straight down on the top of his head. The man's neck seemed to contract under the force, like a turtle trying to hide inside its shell. Bolan grabbed his hair and pitched him forward, out of the way, then turned back to the door.

Pulling it open, Bolan saw a man, wearing a red-and-blue jogging suit, writhing on the floor. He held both hands to his face as blood spurted from his nostrils.

A quick scan up and down the hall told Bolan there was no one else watching. Bending at the knees, he grabbed the man's ankles and pulled him into the restroom. Another Uzi— slung around his shoulder like the first man—slid with him.

As the door swung automatically closed behind him, the bloody-nosed terrorist rose to a sitting position and dropped his hands toward the submachine gun. The Executioner sent a front-knuckle punch into his throat, and the terrorist fell backward, wriggling spasmodically in his final movements before death. Grabbing his ankles again, Bolan dragged him into one of the stalls and up onto the toilet. By seating him on the tank, and dropping his feet into the bowl, he balanced the man so he'd be out of sight with the stall door closed. Pulling the Uzi sling over the dead man's head, he slung it over his own shoulder.

He returned to where the first terrorist lay. Kneeling, he jammed a finger into the side of the man's neck. No pulse—

the hammer fist had been a killing blow, breaking through the skull. Lifting the second Uzi off the ground, Bolan unwound the sling from the man's shoulders, then balanced him in another toilet stall next to his partner.

Bolan stepped up to the sinks and pulled two dozen paper towels from one of the dispensers. Unloading both subguns as he walked to a tall trash can, he dropped the weapons and box mags inside, then covered them with the brown paper.

Bolan looked at his watch. 3:20 p.m. He was running behind schedule. Grimaldi would return to the roof in the OCPD chopper—with the Air Force jets again providing cover noise—at exactly 4:00 p.m. He was timing his exit with the al Qaeda phone call in the hope that the call itself would be a further distraction from what was occurring on the roof.

Leaving the men's room again, Bolan turned the corner down the rear hall and continued to check the second floor. He quickly determined the entire top floor was deserted. The guard he had killed at the stairs, and the two men he'd just left in the men's room were, the only human beings on the second floor of the Liberal Arts building. Which meant everyone had been herded down to the first floor.

Bolan stopped at the stairs leading down. He and Lawford had assumed the hostages would have been spread out in a number of classrooms to make a rescue more difficult. But what if that hadn't been done? Bolan wondered. What if the terrorists had decided to herd all the students to one location and secure them there? Where they'd be easier to keep an eye on?

And easier to blow up when the time came.

Bolan's mind flew back to the blueprints he had studied in the trailer. If the students weren't spread out in the classrooms below, there was only one place large enough to hold them all. And that place was directly below him.

Slowly, quietly, cautiously, the Executioner descended the steps to the first floor. He knew he'd still have to check all of the classrooms on the ground floor. But he'd do so quickly because he knew they'd be empty. He knew where the students were being held now, and he knew that, for whatever reason, they had all been put together.

The four-hundred-odd hostages had to be in the Pegasus Theater.

BOLAN HAD JUST REACHED the ground floor when he heard the footsteps clomping down the far hall on the other side of the building. He looked toward the corner—past a series of tables and chairs in the middle of the hall, and vending machines which lined the wall. The closest place to hide was the office suite behind him, and he ducked past a row of soda machines and through the open glass door.

Dropping to one knee, the Executioner peered back toward the tables and chairs as three men, dressed as college students but carrying AK-47s, walked past the vending machines, speaking in Arabic. None of them looked his way.

Bolan watched the terrorists turn down the hallway that led to the Pegasus Theater. He was about to rise when more footsteps sounded. Twenty feet behind the trio came two more al Qaeda men. One carried an Uzi. The other gripped an MP-5.

The Executioner remained frozen until the men had also turned down the hall toward the theater. Things were definitely busier on the first floor of the building than they were the second, and it appeared that roving, random patrols were moving through the hallways. He would have to do his best to avoid them as he checked each office and classroom to make sure they were unoccupied. There was no getting around it—while he now suspected all of the students had been moved into the theater, he couldn't be sure until he'd seen it with his own eyes. And the exact location of the hostages—*all* of the hostages—was vital to planning a counterattack.

Turning away from the hall, Bolan found himself in the English Creative Studies Department. He hurried in and out of several small offices that circled the reception area, then walked swiftly down a hallway to another set of offices. These, too, were empty. Dropping to a knee again when he returned to the hallway, he checked for signs of the al Qaeda patrols. Seeing none, he sprinted out past the vending machines, ran past the tables and chairs, and turned into an identical setup of offices on the opposite side of the building.

The floor plan was the same. But past the sign announcing Criminal Justice, the Executioner found a major difference to what he'd seen in the other departments.

The first body Bolan came to was just inside the doorway. A thin, older man with a thick head of silver-gray hair lay on his side next to his desk. He might have been an instructor. But he was past the age of being a working cop, and his dress showed no sign of a badge, holster, or any other indication that he was still active. That hadn't stopped al Qaeda from putting a bullet in the side of his head, however.

Bolan stared down at the lifeless body and imagined the scenario. The man had been killed simply to make a point. The al Qaeda killers had known what department they were entering, knew there were likely to be guns. The gray-haired man was the first they encountered, and they wanted everyone to know who was in charge from the very beginning.

But not everyone had taken the hint, the Executioner found, as he made his way through the rest of the offices. He found three more bodies, each looking to have just risen from their desk chairs when the bullets struck. Two of the men wore empty holsters. The third had a badge clipped to his belt.

Bolan started back out toward the hallway. There were at least four victims so far. Innocent, hard-working men who had given their lives trying to stop a terrorist attack and save their students. Silently, he vowed that their murders would be avenged.

Suddenly, Bolan caught a flash of steel. In a microsecond, he realized what was happening and forced his demeanor to change. Throwing up his hands, he turned toward the movement he'd just seen.

Two AK-47s and a Russian Tokarev pistol were aimed at his head, the holes in the ends of the barrels staring at him like a trio of cold eyes.

Bolan widened his eyes and let his mouth fall open, feigning shock, horror and disbelief. Suddenly, three voices were yelling at him in a high-pitched dialect he couldn't understand. He kept the frightened expression on his face, and began shaking his head violently back and forth. "I don't understand!" he said, forcing his voice to tremble with the words. He pointed down to the Bronco emblem on his shirt and said, "Coach! I'm just a football coach!"

The man with the pistol wore a short nylon jacket and the pants to a jogging suit. But he had also donned a kaffiyeh—probably after they'd taken over the building and there was no more need for discretion.

The man in the kaffiyeh shoved the Tokarev hard into the Executioner's face just under his nose. "What are you doing here?" he demanded.

Bolan took a deep breath. "Nothing, I—"

The barrel of the gun struck Bolan on the upper lip. He felt blood drip down his face. "Where did you come from?" the man demanded.

"Look," the Executioner said, the iron taste of his own blood on his lips. "I'm a coach. I just came over here to try to talk one of the professors into passing my star linebacker. I was in the men's room when you guys—"

"You lie!" The Tokarev hit him just above the ear this time. "We checked all bathrooms!"

Bolan's hands were over his head. Now he lowered them slightly and turned them palms up. "All I can tell you," he said, "is nobody checked the one I was in." He nodded over his shoulder toward the Criminal Justice offices. "There's a faculty men's room back there. That's where I was."

The terrorist with the pistol stared hard at the Executioner. Bolan could practically see the man's brain working. The whole football coach story seemed more plausible than when he'd invented it. With all of the shooting that had gone on in the Criminal Justice offices, and the confusion that would have accompanied it, overlooking one man in a restroom hardly seemed impossible.

The Executioner watched the man watch him. The terrorist's eyes burned holes of hatred through his own, searching for any sign of a lie. Bolan wondered why the man was going to so much trouble. With hundreds of hostages already, al Qaeda hardly had a need for one more. The easiest thing to do would be to kill him.

But that wasn't what happened. The terrorist leader barked orders in Arabic to his two men. They stepped forward, each grabbing one of the Executioner's arms. Turning him, they began marching Bolan past the tables, chairs and vending machines toward the hall he knew led to the Pegasus Theater.

Bolan didn't resist.

While they'd been talking, the Executioner had studied all three men carefully. The two men with the rifles wore no pistols he could see. But one of them had what looked like a sheathed Kindjal hanging from a black leather belt he had buckled over his gray sweat pants. It looked like it had a blade roughly ten inches long.

The man with the pistol followed, the barrel of the Tokarev occasionally hitting Bolan in the back of the head to encourage him onward. The Executioner watched the two men at his sides out of the corners of his eyes. He knew he'd have to take them all down before they got to the theater. Once they had him there, while he might not be helpless, his chances of overcoming the entire terrorist cell without hostages being shot or blown up would be next to nothing.

Just before they reached the corner that led to the Pegasus Theater, Bolan stumbled. Letting out a short gasp of pain, he stopped suddenly, reached down and grabbed his right knee. His sudden halt brought the men to a stop at his sides, and their voices began again, sounding angry.

The Executioner felt the Tokarev strike him across the back of the neck. He'd been expecting it. The man in the kaffiyeh stepped around to the front and jammed the Russian weapon under Bolan's chin. "What you are doing?" he demanded.

"My knee," Bolan said, straightening slightly. "Goes out on me sometimes. I told you I was a football coach. I—"

The Tokarev struck him across the face.

As soon as he felt the cold steel meet his skin, the Executioner reached up and snatched the pistol out of the terrorist's hand. Bringing it around backhanded, he caught the man hard on the temple. At the same time he was breaking the terrorist leader's cheekbone, he stepped forward and to the side. Reaching out, he grasped the grip of the Kindjal in the other man's belt.

Bolan jerked the long, razor-sharp blade from leather and dragged the edge across the throat of the man who had worn it. Moving quickly, he shifted his angle of attack slightly, then cut the throat of the man who had held his other arm.

In less than two seconds, all three men were on the ground, two of them drowning in their own blood.

The Executioner looked up and down the hall and saw no one else. But he knew he didn't have much time. Another of the roving patrols might show up at any time, and if they saw him from a distance they would sound the alarm. If that happened, the hostages were as good as dead.

Bolan checked his wristwatch and saw that Grimaldi would drop the helicopter to the roof again in four minutes. If Bolan had not shown his face by the time the Air Force jets flew over, the Stony Man pilot had orders to take off again rather than risk alerting the terrorists.

Bolan glanced down the hall to the intersecting walkway that led to the theater. The bottom line was that he had to know for sure that the hostages were being held in the theater, or his entire soft probe would have been worthless.

The soldier grabbed the two men whose throats he had cut and dragged them into the nearest office. He lifted the man in the kaffiyeh and took him into the same office. The blow to the temple had left a large discolored spot on the side of his face, and his eyes stared wide open in death.

The Executioner looked down at the three men. He needed something to hide his features long enough for him to take a quick glance into the theater.

That something was the kaffiyeh.

Grabbing the headdress, Bolan let the tails fall around his face. Then, lifting one of the AK-47s, more for cover than protection, he hurried down the hall.

Bolan walked quickly past the blood on the tile where he'd cut the terrorist's throats. There was no time to clean it up. He'd have to hope it either went unnoticed, or was attributed to the deaths of some of the hostages.

He checked his watch as he turned the corner toward the Pegasus Theater. He had less than two minutes before the scheduled pickup on the roof.

A half-dozen al Qaeda men were loitering outside the front of the theater, talking and waiting for whatever would happen after the phone call. Bolan kept his face averted as he passed, stooping slightly and hoping that his height would not be noticed. When he reached the nearest door, he cracked it open and looked in.

One terrorist stood just inside the door. But his back was turned to the Executioner as he looked out over the theater seats filled with fear-frozen students. A dozen more al Qaeda men stood on stage bearing rifles and submachine guns, and more were stationed at each exit and up and down the aisles amid the seats. Bolan could see no sign of explosives, which meant nothing. A bomb could be hidden any number of places.

Bolan estimated the terrorists at around thirty. He closed the door. Turning, he walked casually back down the hall in the direction from which he'd come, again keeping his face away from the men stationed outside. And again, luck was with him. They paid him no attention.

That luck ran out, however, as soon as Bolan rounded the corner away from the theater.

He had barely one minute left before Grimaldi returned to the roof. He had planned to sprint toward the stairs as soon as he was clear but, as he turned to his left, he ran headlong into two more terrorists.

The duo stopped in their tracks when they saw Bolan. They seemed to know immediately that something was out of place. But the kaffiyeh confused them for the split second Bolan needed, and by the time their brains had processed the fact that the man before them was not one of them, the Executioner had caved in both of their heads with the wooden stock of his rifle.

They fell to the floor, dead before they hit.

Bolan had thirty seconds left. He didn't have enough time to hide more bodies. But if he left the men where they'd be found, he might as well just go back and shoot all of the college kids himself.

Slinging the AK-47 around his neck, the Executioner bent and lifted one of the terrorists to his right shoulder, the other to his left in a double fireman's carry. Then, bearing what he guessed to be well over three hundred pounds, he began running toward the stairs.

Bolan's quadriceps screamed as he raced up the stairs. When he reached the second floor, he turned toward the steps leading up onto the roof, wondering as he ran how he could get the door open without dropping the men.

He couldn't. At least not without dropping one of them. So, when he reached the steel door, he wasted no time letting the man on his left shoulder slip to the wall, then reached out to grab the doorknob.

As he did, the Executioner saw the watch on his forearm. He had exactly twelve seconds left.

Bolan twisted the doorknob, shoved the door open and held it with his foot as he lifted the dead terrorist again. He raced up the steps as the sound of jet planes nearing the building roared through the stairwell. At the top of the steps he dropped the same man he had dropped before, shot out his hand, and ripped open the door.

Three seconds.

The roar of the jets was almost deafening as Bolan stumbled through the doorway onto the roof. The helicopter hovered overhead, and the line had already been dropped. With only one harness available—bringing dead bodies back had not been anticipated—Bolan dropped the men and buckled himself in. Then, grabbing the bodies at his feet by their belt buckles, he held on as he was hauled up into the air.

A moment later, hands were reaching out of the side of the chopper. The regular OCPD police pilot was riding with Grimaldi, and he pulled as the Executioner pushed the dead terrorists through the doorway, then climbed in himself. The helicopter took off straight up for several hundred feet, then began to descend toward the UCO football field.

Bolan's whole body felt as if it had caught fire. Carrying the dead men up two flights of stairs, then holding on to them as they rose toward the chopper had taken its toll. He looked at his coach's shirt and slacks, and saw the blood of the dead men mixed with that dripping from his own face where the Tokarev had struck

As he caught his breath, Jack Grimaldi looked over his shoulder. "Have fun?" he asked with a pleasant smile.

12

The al Qaeda phone call had come, as promised, as Bolan returned to the command trailer in the parking lot. Linked into the same UCO PD line the terrorists had called earlier, Lawford had taken the call himself.

Recter stood next to the desk when Bolan walked in. He and Lawford were speaking and, though still too far away to hear their words, it was apparent that an argument of some kind was in progress. By the time he got into hearing range all he heard was Lawford's irritated, *"Now, dammit!"*

Recter turned, stared daggers at Bolan, then stalked off.

"Our friendly neighborhood 'lawyer with a gun' isn't exactly in love with you," Lawford told the Executioner as he sat down.

"It's just as well," Bolan said. "He's not my type."

Lawford let a short chuckle escape his chest. "Seems the federal bureaucracy was at work while you were inside. The feds have taken over. But instead of the FBI the President has specified that *you* be in charge."

Bolan knew that had to have been Brognola's work, behind the scenes. "Tell me about the phone call," he said.

"No big surprises," Lawford said. "Along with the call we

got a fax. And all the major news networks got it, too. There are 131 men al Qaeda wants released."

"They know it won't happen," Bolan said.

Lawford nodded in agreement. "They're also demanding the immediate withdrawal of American troops from the Middle East." The OSBI director ran a hand through his thinning hair, and the stress on his face seemed to increase. "And like you said, they want TV coverage."

"The networks on their way yet?" Bolan asked.

"Got here while you were still inside the building," Lawford said. "We've got them waiting on the other side of the campus. I understand from the officers over there it's like trying to keep a herd of cattle corralled during a thunderstorm."

Bolan nodded. An idea was beginning to form in his brain. "Keep them there for now. They may come in handy eventually."

Lawford looked at Bolan quizzically, but he let the statement pass without question. "I just sent Recter over there to take charge of them," he said. "He got his tail caught on the fence over it but he's out of our way," Lawford continued. "The guy on the phone—called himself Ali—demanded no fewer than three, no more than four, cameras. Two cameramen and one journalist with each camera. If anyone's armed, they blow up the building right then."

Bolan frowned. "Do we have any confirmation on explosives yet?"

Lawford shook his head. "No. You see anything inside?"

Bolan shook his head. "No. But that doesn't mean anything. I wasn't able to look carefully, and it would be easy to hide enough C-4, or Semtex, or any number of other combustibles with enough power to take out a building this size."

Lawford put both hands on his knees and arched his back. "You have a plan in mind, I hope?" he said.

"One's forming," Bolan replied. He looked around the trailer. "The first thing we do is move this command post to a larger room. I want to meet with every SWAT team member you've got on the scene."

"University president's already made the field house available to us," Lawford said. "They were evacuating everybody when Recter was there." The man's eyes dropped to the blood-splattered shirt Bolan still wore. "You got a change with you or you want me to send somebody for more clothes?"

"Don't worry about it," the Executioner said. "For what I have in mind, the clothes will bring themselves."

Lawford looked puzzled again. But again, he let it pass.

"Do whatever you have to do to get the SWAT teams to the field house," Bolan said. "Then get on the horn to Recter. Tell him to pick four of the major news crews and send them over there, too." He reached down, lifted the blueprint of the Liberal Arts building from the desk top and began rolling it up. "And we'll need some regular officers, or maybe some of your agents. Half a dozen should do it." He turned toward the end of the trailer. "I'll head on over and start setting up for the briefing."

BOLAN GOT OUT OF A POLICE vehicle and followed Chief Theodore into the field house. They cut through the front offices, passed a huge, well-quipped weight-training room and a room with wrestling mats covering the floor, then pushed through the doors onto the basketball court.

Men in a variety of blue-and-black jumpsuits and fatigues

had begun arriving as the Executioner wheeled a portable easel out in front of the bleachers. Unrolling the blueprint of the Liberal Arts building, he slipped it under the clips at the top and smoothed it against the wooden backboard. Turning, he saw that Theodore had taken charge of directing the men to seats in the bleachers. Lawford walked in and took a seat next to the UCO chief in the first row.

Bolan looked out over the hardened faces seated before him. SWAT. Special Weapons and Tactics. They were the hard-core shooters, door-and-ass kickers; men who were willing to take on the challenges from which other cops shied away.

Clearing his throat, Bolan said, "Men, I'm not going to lie to you. Two hours from now, some of you will be dead." He paused to let it sink in. Not a muscle in the bleachers moved. "I think everyone here has already figured that out for himself. But I want to make it very clear. This is a suicide mission on al Qaeda's part. They intend to die right along with the hostages."

There were murmurs of acknowledgment throughout the bleachers.

"We're going to tackle this job in two assaults," Bolan explained. "One right after the other. The first will consist of twelve men posing as cameramen and reporters. This team will include me, and eleven others. It's strictly volunteer, and anyone wanting to opt out shouldn't feel ashamed."

Again, the men in the bleachers remained still. No one was backing away.

"This initial team will have to be completely unarmed. No hideout guns, nothing. We'll be searched, and they've promised to blow the whole place sky high if they find so much as a pocketknife, or have any other reason to believe we're anything other than what we say we are—newsmen." Turning to his side, he walked slowly in front of the rows of men in the risers. "My plan is fairly simple. We go in and set up just like real camera crews. Then, when you see me move, everyone goes for the nearest terrorist's weapon. It doesn't matter how you get their guns, just that you get them as quickly as possible, and start shooting.

"Team Two will consist of everybody who isn't on Team One," Bolan said. He walked back to the easel. "You'll move in from hiding as soon as you hear the first shots inside." He pointed to the blueprint. "OKC, I want you guys dropping down on the roof and taking the second floor. I went in that way earlier, and the rooms upstairs were deserted. But we can't count on them still being that way now."

"You leave the door unlocked for us?" somebody quipped and the rest of the men laughed.

Bolan nodded. Humor was one of the ways such men dealt with the stress of knowing they might be about to die. "I left the door unlocked," he said. "And the lights on for you, too."

The men laughed again. They could sense Bolan was one of them. They knew he was the alpha male—the natural leader.

Bolan outlined the plan of how they would secure the building after Team One had done its part.

"By the time Team One comes out it'll all be over," he said. "The hostages will either be safe or we'll all be dead."

Bolan finished the briefing. "I'll leave it to your individual team leaders to select the locations where you set up. Grab one of the UCO cops to help you if you like. They'll know the campus. Just make sure no one can see you from the Liberal Arts building before it's time to move in." He stopped, took in a short breath, then said, "Anyone wanting to volunteer for the camera squad—Team One—stay where you are. The rest of you—Team Two—go outside and get organized."

Several of the men had started to rise as it became obvious that the briefing was about to end. But now they sat back down. None of the other officers moved, either. Every last man was volunteering for the hazardous, unarmed, Team One.

They were all willing to die.

He turned toward Lawford and Theodore. Beckoning them, he saw that both men were smiling.

When they reached Bolan, he said, "There are only twelve slots open on Team One. And I plan on taking one of them myself." He glanced back to the risers. "You know these men better than I do. Pick the best eleven for me."

"You don't need eleven," Lawford said. "Just nine."

The Executioner stood, waiting, knowing already what the OSBI director and UCO chief had in mind. He looked at the gray hair on both men's heads, the wrinkles and battle scars on their faces. "Gentlemen," he said, "with all due respect—"

But Lawford had been prepared for an argument. "Look," he said, "neither Theo nor I are quite as fast as we used to be. And we're not quite as strong. But we're hardly ready for the Old Cops' Home, either." He stopped to clear his throat, and that gave Theodore a chance to step in.

"This gig doesn't call for any long-distance running," the UCO chief said. "It's a matter of surprising the hell out of them, taking their guns away and killing them. Lawford and I have both seen a lot more action than these kids—" he nodded his head toward the bleachers "—have had time to see yet. We know everything turns to chaos once the first shot's been fired, and we know how to deal with it. Besides, like you said, it's all going to all be over—one way or another—in a matter of minutes." The serious look he'd had on his face so far now softened. "We won't have time to get tired."

Before Bolan could respond Lawford launched into phase two of his argument. "And don't forget our man on the inside—Professor Williams. He's smart and, if he's still alive, he'll be waiting for something like this. But he's been away from the game for a while, and he's not likely to recognize any of these young guys. But he'll know me."

"And he knows me, too," Theodore said. "For that matter, there still might be a few cops or Criminal Justice students alive in there. They'll recognize me from around the campus."

Bolan shook his head, more in amazement than refusal. "How long did it take you two to rehearse this act?" he asked.

"We came up with it in the short time you were talking," Theodore said. "Which should prove to you how fast we think."

"Okay," Bolan said. "Go pick nine good men." He shook his head again, then added, "And you might try to get at least a few under the age of fifty. You never know when somebody might have to do a little running."

13

Carl Jennings sat behind his desk, staring at the computer screen in front of him. His head ached, and his stomach felt as if it would turn itself inside out any second. Part of his illness was the hangover from the night before—he and Moshe Singer had sat at the Shamrock, drinking and talking, until the place closed. But the alcohol could not account for all of the sickness or anxiety Jennings felt at the moment.

A good deal of it came from the fight going on within his soul.

Sweat broke out on his face as he sat there, trying to figure out the answer to his moral dilemma. When Singer had first sat down after returning from the restroom, and it became apparent that he knew Jennings had found the Mossad ID, he had thought for a moment that the Israeli agent might kill him. Singer had laughed when he'd noticed the concern on his face.

"You need to remember, my young friend," the Mossad man had said, "that our nations are friends. We do not hurt our friends, only our enemies, is that not true?"

Jennings had still been in a state of half-drunken shock. He remembered nodding dumbly.

"Israel, the U.S., Great Britain," Singer had said. "We are

all in this War Against Terrorism together, and we must stay together, or we will perish."

Jennings picked a pencil up off his desk and stuck the eraser in his mouth, tasting the rubber on his tongue and biting down into the wood with his teeth. He remembered that it had not been too much later that he had blurted out the fact that he worked for Homeland Security, and he remembered the shocked look that had come over Singer's face. But the Israeli was an old hand at the game, and his surprise had not come from the intelligence connection but rather at the mere coincidence of it all.

"Who would have guessed it?" he laughed. "An old Jew and a young Jew meeting, becoming friends, and learning they are in the same line of work?" Singer was surprised, all right. But he'd have been just as surprised if they'd both turned out to be doctors or plumbers or bankers.

Jennings bit down harder on the pencil. He remembered apologizing for his nosiness. Singer had said, "Think nothing of it. It is our job to do such things." He had chuckled again, then remarked that maybe he was getting too old for such work himself. Here he was, an intelligence officer with close to forty years of experience, and a brand-new agent from another country had fingered him before he'd had even the slightest hint of who he was drinking with.

That statement had restored Jennings' self-respect, at least partially, and he had paid for the next round of drinks.

Taking the pencil out of his mouth, he opened the top right-hand drawer of his desk and rummaged until he round a half-empty roll of Tums. Popping four of the tablets into his mouth, his thoughts returned to Moshe Singer as he began to chew.

As soon as the Mossad agent had learned that he was sitting with a fellow spy—and Jennings had been too ashamed to admit that he had yet to take his first step into the field—he had begun to open up in a different way. He told fascinating stories about the cold war between American and the old Soviet Union, and the role Israel had played.

As the night wore on, Frank came and went with more martinis and Pernod, and somewhere along the line Moshe Singer had mentioned the current political friction between the U.S. and Israel. Jennings had not been aware of any such problems. But, then, he was hardly in the loop. He suspected he had shown his lack of knowledge on his face because Singer had said, "Oh yes. It comes and goes, of course. Politicians are the bane of the intelligence officer's existence—and it is the same in all countries, I think." Then he went on to tell Jennings about a joint endeavor between the U.S and Israel that had been aborted when the U.S. Senate voted down funding.

"What was the project?" Very tipsy, Jennings had spoken the words before he realized the question might seem unprofessional. Was he being indiscreet? Did he sound like the rookie paper pusher that he knew himself to be?

If Singer thought so, or was offended by the question, he didn't show it. "We had combined forces with the CIA—and I suppose your agency would have been involved eventually had it continued—to assess security at nuclear power plants in both the United States and Israel. It was to be a joint effort, with the U.S. setting up the framework for the evaluation." The older man tapped his fingers along the top of the table, then lifted his drink and took a sip. "The United States was to put together a checklist of sorts that would be used to identify potential security weaknesses around nuclear power plants in both of our countries. Israel was to prepare several teams of agents to portray terrorists who would attempt to infiltrate these facilities." He paused, took another drink, then smiled the wry smile Jennings had come to expect just before he said something mildly sarcastic. "In other words, both countries would do what they did best. America would provide the money and technical assistance to set things up. And we Israelis have skin that looks closer to that of Arab terrorists." Downing the last of his Pernod, he tapped his glass on the table and turned toward the bar.

Frank heard the sound, looked up and nodded.

"I know little about computers," the Israeli agent said as the bartender brought them fresh drinks. "But it is my understanding that they were to play some part in it all, too." He nodded to Frank as the man set their glasses down, then shrugged yet again. "It makes no difference now. The mission is dead to Israel. We are far too poor a nation to do such an expensive evaluation on our own." He lifted his glass. "To the death of all politicians, in all countries, in all the world," he said in toast.

Drunk as he had been, Jennings still remembered feeling the hair stand up on the back of his neck as he tapped his martini glass against Singer's Pernod. He had not told his new friend that not only was the nuclear power plant evaluation still on in the U.S.—he was part of it. But in his inebriated state, he had asked the man if it would help if he could somehow secure a copy of the checklist.

He suspected Singer had guessed his new friend might have access to the list at that point, because the old man had pursed his lips and shook his head sadly. "Do not risk your career on such a thing," he said. "The checklist would be of no use to us without specific examples of how it is used—how it is interpreted, so to speak. The U.S. was to provide these examples, and we were to use them as guidelines for our own efforts in Israel." His eyes lit up with a hint of excitement, as if for a second he believed the mission was still on. "We could use each other as a cross-check then, don't you see? And the final test would be the Mossad—pretending to be terrorists—trying to find any security weak spots that remained." As he finished, the light in his eyes died again, and he looked as if he had aged twenty years.

Returning to the present, Jennings sat back in his chair and stuck the pencil back between his teeth. What should he do? The easy answer was to keep his mouth shut and never let on that the information Singer needed was right at his fingertips.

Even with his hands clasped in his lap, Jennings felt them tremble. Giving *any* intelligence information to the agent of another county—even an ally—without authorization was not only against policy but against the law. Even providing the checklist itself could get him fired. But to also give the Israeli a specific U.S. site which had been evaluated, well, that was another step toward treason.

He had sworn before God and man that he would never betray his country, and he never intended to do so. But wasn't there a bigger picture that needed looking at here? A greater good that could be served, perhaps? Special circumstances? Forget the fact that Israel was the land of his forefathers—even with his new racial awareness he could not allow such thinking to enter into his decision. What was pertinent was that Israel was one of America's closest allies. And the only true ally the U.S. had in the Middle East. The project had originally included them. Except for the senatorial wavering, it still would.

Moshe Singer was right. Politicians were the natural enemies of intelligence officers.

If Israeli nuclear power plants weren't safe, the entire Middle East was a ticking time bomb. Nuclear blasts had no respect for national boundaries, and an incident in Israel was bound to bleed over into any number of the Arab countries surrounding it. The whole world would be at risk if that happened.

Jennings tossed four more Tums into his mouth. It was another of the downfalls of bureaucracy, he realized. The powerful few—like those U.S. senators—made selfish decisions that were detrimental to the rest of the world.

Jennings knew politics and bureaucracy had kept him frozen in his boring, dead-end, paper-pushing position.

He swallowed the Tums and realized his stomach had already settled. His headache was gone, too. He lifted his hands and looked down at them. Steady as a rock. It had to be because he knew, in his heart, that he had finally made his decision. He knew what he would do—*had to do*—to serve the interests of his country. Sometimes there really was a greater good than the one others saw. Sometimes you had to break the rules—even the law—to do what was right.

Hell, Carl Jennings smiled to himself. James Bond did it all the time.

The smile faded as quickly as it had come, however, as Jennings realized that if he got caught he would lose his job, and might even end up in prison. But that was part of the risk—part of doing the right thing. You had to be willing to suffer the consequences if you got caught by those who didn't understand.

Excitement began to flow through the young DHS man's veins. Until now, he had not seen any way he could help his country in the job he was in. But now he had a chance to save the U.S. from the selfish acts of a few immoral politicians who thought nothing of risking a nuclear explosion in order to further their own careers.

Leaning forward, Jennings punched the start button on his printer.

A moment later, the diagram of a nuclear power plant in North Dakota came sliding out into the tray.

14

The Executioner stood at the door to the coach's office in the front of the field house, looking at a face several million people watched every night on TV. But they never saw her glare the way she did at Bolan. And they probably never suspected that the sweet, innocent face with the flaming red hair, and vanilla ice-cream-colored complexion, even knew some of the four-letter words she was using.

The truth was, she had a mouth foul enough to make a Hell's Angel blush.

There were three other women in the coach's office, as well as eight men. The women still wore the clothes in which they'd arrived, but the men were all dressed in blue-and-gold University of Central Oklahoma track suits which fit poorly, and looked completely out of place on their lumpy, overweight bodies. Six of Lawford's OSBI agents stood between Bolan and the shouting newsmen and -women, holding them back.

"You ever heard of the First Amendment, you son of a bitch?" the redhead screamed at Bolan. The news crews had learned they'd be held at the field house instead of interviewing al Qaeda men in the Liberal Arts building. "You ever heard of freedom of the press?"

"I'm sorry for any inconvenience this may have caused you," Bolan said.

"Inconvenience?" the redhead shouted. "*Inconvenience?* What you're doing is against the Constitution! I want your badge number and I want it now."

Bolan told her the truth. "I don't have a badge."

"Give it to me!" she screamed, trying to claw her way around two OSBI men who were taking the brunt of her anger as they kept her restrained. "I'll have your job!"

The Executioner was honest again. "I don't have a job, either," he said, then turned and walked out of the office and back to the gym. In the closet in the same office, he had found a pair of gray slacks, a blue blazer and a white sport shirt that belonged to someone about his size. The shoes were a little tight, he thought as he opened the door and stepped back out onto the basketball court, but beggars couldn't be choosers. Especially when every second delay might mean the slaughter of hostages.

Team Two, consisting of all the SWAT team members who had not been chosen to pose as newsmen, had left the building to set up. They would take up positions as close as they could get to their entry points in the Liberal Arts building. None of them would start to move until the first shots were fired from inside the Pegasus Theater.

Bolan stopped just short of the men waiting on him. In his heart, he knew that Team Two could be nothing but a cleanup squad. Whatever was going to happen would happen long before they had time to arrive. He looked at the eleven men standing before him. It was up to them.

Eight of the members of Team One were dressed in the

clothing the male newsmen had worn. The ninth had traded garb with one of the undercover cops at the site. Theodore had hurried half a block down to his office, then returned wearing a plaid sport coat and cream-colored polo shirt.

Lawford still wore his suit. The only change he had made was to loosen his tie.

"Everybody ready?" Bolan asked.

Eleven heads nodded back at him.

"Last chance to back out," Bolan said. "No shame in it if you want to."

His remark was met with silence.

"One more question," Bolan said. "Anybody decide to go against my orders and try to sneak a gun or knife through?"

Heads shook back and forth.

"Because if you do, they'll find it," the Executioner said. "And when they find it, they'll probably keep their promise of blowing things up right then. At the very least, they'll kill you." He looked from face to face, making eye contact with each man. "And if by chance they don't, *I will.*"

These were not the kind of men who showed fear of their commanders. But the Executioner could see in their eyes that he had their respect. If any of them planned to defy his order of going in unarmed, they would have done it openly.

"Then let's move out," Bolan said. He turned and led them out of the building.

AS HE NEARED THE GLASS entryway, the Executioner could see the terrified faces of six young college students—three boys, three girls. Directly behind them but less distinctly, he could make out the features of men holding guns to the back of the kids' heads. Like the ones he'd already encountered, the terrorists Bolan saw now were dressed much like their hostages. But they had added a touch here and there after taking over the building. On one man, the Executioner saw another checkered kaffiyeh. Another had a topped his blue jeans with a camouflage BDU blouse.

As he drew nearer and saw the faces behind the students more clearly, Bolan was struck by the similarity in the ages of the prisoners and the captors.

The only real difference the Executioner noticed was in the eyes. Those of the hostages reflected horror. The eyes of the al Qaeda men looked crazed.

"Halt!" a voice on the other side of the glass shouted out as the Executioner reached for the door.

He froze in place. "Bill Dexter," he said. "FOX News. This is——"

"Silence!" the same voice shouted through the glass. A hand reached out around a blond girl in a pink sweater and pushed the door open. "Enter one at a time!" came the order.

Bolan stepped through the door and was immediately grabbed and slammed face-first into the wall. He spread his arms and legs as hands moved up and down his body searching for any kind of weapon. When they found the pens and notebook they were jerked out for inspection, then returned to his pocket. A second later, he was grabbed by the shoulders and spun back around away from the wall.

Two young men stood in front of Bolan. One wore blue jeans and a plain white T-shirt. A short stubble of hair covered his scalp, and he had an equally skimpy mustache and goatee. His eyes narrowed menacingly. "Go with him," he ordered Bolan in nearly unaccented English, hooking a thumb toward the other terrorist at his side.

The second man wore baggy white pants and bright green running shoes. Like most of the other al Qaeda men, his weapon—a 9 mm Uzi—was slung over his shoulder. But he kept his right hand on the grip, his finger on the trigger and the barrel pointed at Bolan as he reached out and grabbed the Executioner's arm.

As the terrorist jerked him away from the wall, Bolan took note of the knife handle sticking out of the sheath on his belt. He was taking in all of the details about the men that he could. One of these finer points might determine the fate of four hundred lives.

As the terrorist walked him farther down the hall, Bolan saw Lawford being jerked inside the building and thrown against the wall to be searched. The terrorist at his side led Bolan halfway down the hall, then stopped him between the tables and vending machines. The Executioner glanced toward the Criminal Justice offices on the other side of the building. If the dead al Qaeda men he'd left there earlier had been found, he could see no sign of it. He wasn't surprised. Things were happening at an incredible pace for everyone. He doubted any of the men he'd killed had even been missed yet.

One by one, each of the SWAT-team-newsmen were pulled inside the building and searched. The four shoulder-mounted TV cameras received as much attention as the men. The terrorists practically took them apart to make sure no weapons were hidden inside. As they worked, Bolan continued to watch carefully, studying each of the individual.

Gradually, other members of Team One joined Bolan amid

the tables and vending machines. Each man had been assigned a guard, and each guard was armed with a rifle or submachine gun. The security strategy was obvious to Bolan. In addition to the precautions already in place, each of the television journalists would have his own babysitter while in the building. And that could be used to Team One's advantage. The guards would stick close to the men they'd been assigned. And close was the name of the game when going up against a gunman with bare hands.

Finally, twenty-four men—twelve terrorists, eleven cops posing as TV newsmen, and the Executioner—stood in front of the vending machines. The man with the close-cropped hair barked orders in Arabic, and the men holding the six students at gunpoint in front of the entryway began backing away from the glass and heading toward the theater.

The man in the white T-shirt said, "My men will carry your cameras. You will be taken to the location where the prisoners are being held and assigned positions from which to work. Then your equipment will be returned to you. You will film our leader who is about to speak." Turning away again, he shouted orders to his men. At the other end of the hall, four of the terrorists let their rifles fall to the end of the slings around their shoulders, lifted the cameras from the floor where they'd been set for inspection and started down the hall.

15

The curtains had been drawn on the stage, and the bare bricks along the back wall could be seen. A large white clock had been mounted to the brick, and its white face stared out toward the seats as if to remind everyone in the theater that they were running out of time. Stacked to both sides of the clock were props, and the walls of a set, for some upcoming play.

But the current drama was all center stage as Bolan was walked down the left hand aisle. The students crowded into the seats whispered quietly as the Executioner looked up to see a man—probably in his late thirties—patiently waiting at the microphone. His eyes glared at Bolan and the other men entering the auditorium. He was dressed in a curious cross between Middle East and West. On his head was a kaffiyeh, and below his black-bearded face he wore a robe that ended at the knees. Beneath the hem of the robe, green BDU pants were tucked into black combat boots. The robe was cinched at the waist by a wide leather belt. A pistol of some kind hung in a worn brown flap holster on his right hip. On his left, extending from the top of a leather sheath, was the odd-looking grip of a Katar—an ancient push-dagger design that incorporated a transverse bar as well as wrist reinforcements. Slung across his back was what had become as much a symbol of terrorism as an upraised fist was of anger: an AK-47.

Seated in chairs directly behind the podium were three terrified girls. Behind each girl stood a terrorist, and each one had a pistol pressed to the back of the girl's head.

"Stop! You work here! " the man in the green shoes ordered as Bolan headed down the aisle toward the stage. They were the first words the Executioner had heard come out of this mouth. Thickly accented, they had the ring of something the terrorist had learned to say phonetically.

Bolan did as he was told, then turned to see that Lawford's and Theodore's handlers had stopped them, as well. So had the men escorting the "MSNBC" team, just behind them. The curly-haired Oklahoma Highway Patrolmen, the power lifter from the War Acres PD, and another SWAT cop from Cleveland County stopped next to them.

Across the auditorium, in the other aisle, the terrorists halted the other two camera teams at roughly the same distance from the stage. Bolan frowned. They needed to spread out as much as possible to be effective. If two teams were jammed together in the aisles, their effectiveness was essentially cut by half. The odds were already against them, and the Executioner didn't intend to let them be stacked any higher.

"We don't have room to all work here," Bolan told the man in the green shoes. "We're going to move down toward the front." He started that way, but the hand reached out and grabbed his arm again. Words he couldn't understand came sputtering out of the al Qaeda man's mouth.

A moment later, the terrorist with the closely cropped hair

and beard came running down the aisle. "What is the problem?" he demanded to know.

Bolan told him. "Six men can't maneuver in this aisle," he said in an exasperated tone of voice.

"You will have to find a way," the man said.

"Well, there *isn't* a way!" Bolan said, hoping to sound like a spoiled news star who was used to getting whatever he wanted. "If you want your message sent out properly, you're going to have to let one of our crews move forward, or backward, or somewhere else." He crossed his arms and stared the young man in the eyes.

For a second, the terrorist gripped the Uzi slung over his shoulder as if he were going to raise it and shoot Bolan then and there. Then something behind the Executioner caught his eye, and he looked up. Bolan twisted that way, and saw the man on stage shaking his head back and forth. His eyes fell forward down the aisle, and he nodded.

A moment later, Bolan, Lawford and Theodore were relocating closer to the stage. Across the room, another camera crew was moving forward as well. Bolan's gamble had paid off. The four teams were spread out as effectively as possible to cover the entire theater.

As Lawford and Theodore busied themselves pretending they knew how to get the camera rolling, as Bolan scanned the auditorium. Besides the al Qaeda guards assigned individually to him and the other members of Team One, more terrorists were scattered throughout the seats—standing, weapons ready, among the seated hostages. He didn't have time to count them, but he guessed at thirty, and made a rough mental note of their positions.

Behind him, Bolan heard Lawford whisper, "Left side, third row from the front, fourth seat from the wall."

"No speak!" the OSBI man's guard shouted. But it was clear the man had no idea what Lawford had said. Casually, he turned to the seat the director had indicated and saw a burly man roughly Lawford's age staring over his shoulder at them with battle-hardened eyes. Gary Williams.

Theodore had the camera on his shoulder, and Lawford finally found the on switch. The lights on the camera lit up.

Bolan looked at the other crew so he knew the charade couldn't go on much longer. The terrorists would soon begin to notice that none of the crews had the foggiest idea what they were doing.

The curly-haired trooper caught Bolan's eye and gave him a short grim nod. The Executioner turned to the other two camera teams and got similar "good to go" signs. Finally, he turned back to where Professor Williams sat, still staring at them.

The man with the shaved head, white beard and bushy mustache looked Bolan squarely in the eye and nodded as well.

The Executioner reached under his blue blazer, drew one of the pens from his shirt pocket, and drove it up through the eye socket and into the brain of the al Qaeda man wearing the green running shoes.

Before anyone realized what had happened, Bolan reached down with his other hand and jerked the knife on the man's belt from its sheath. As the terrorist began to fall, the Executioner reached down to grab the barrel of his Uzi. The razor-edged knife blade sliced through the sling around the man's shoulder, and less than two seconds after the pen had killed the man, the Executioner was holding the submachine gun.

The shock wore off the hostages and terrorists as suddenly as it had come upon them. As Bolan flipped the Uzi around in his hands, shrieks and shouts broke out, and the theater turned to pandemonium.

As he readjusted his grip on the subgun, Bolan saw Theodore raise the camera over his head with both hands. He brought it down with all his might on the head of the terrorist who'd been guarding him.

Next to Theodore, Lawford drove his fist into the face of his guard. Before the man could retaliate, the Executioner had flipped the safety on the Uzi, pointed the weapon at the al Qaeda man and squeezed the trigger. Lawford and Theodore dropped down to retrieve the weapons the al Qaeda men had dropped. Lawford came up with an AK-47. Theodore raised another Uzi.

"Get down!" Bolan shouted at the top of his lungs, hoping the students and faculty in the seats would hear him. The chair backs were hardly bulletproof, but the hostages would be safer out of sight on the floor. He scanned the chaos all around him and saw that the other three camera teams had gone into action. They were at various levels of disarming their terrorist guards, and two more of the al Qaeda men had fallen. But none of the good guys were down. At least not yet.

Bolan knew the girls on the stage were in the most immediate danger. As he whirled back toward them, he caught a glimpse of Professor Williams's shaved head rising from his seat. The man had both hands jammed down the front of the faded blue jeans he wore beneath a plaid lumberjack shirt.

The Executioner faced the stage. The man behind the podium had disappeared. But he wasn't Bolan's most immediate target—the terrorists behind the girls were. Bringing the Uzi up toward the chairs on stage, Bolan lined up the sights as quickly as he could.

The man to the far right was looking out over the audience, still in awe, as if he had forgotten than his first task should things go bad was to murder the innocent girl.

The Executioner took advantage of that moment of indecision. He squeezed the trigger and felt the open breach of the Israeli subgun slam shut. A semiauto 9 mm round shot from the stubby barrel, over the shoulder of the dark-haired girl, and into the left eye of the man behind her.

The terrorist's head exploded and he fell back, away from the girl. Swinging the Uzi to his left, Bolan raised the sights again.

Like his confederate, the next man had been looking out at what was happening in the audience, and the Executioner had a clear, and easy, shot. But as he began to squeeze the trigger, the man suddenly hunched low behind the girl.

Seeing only bare brick in his sight pattern now, Bolan let up on the trigger. For a second, the terrorist was completely hidden. Then the hand holding the pistol snaked around the side of the girl's neck and jammed the barrel into her temple.

The only chance he had, Bolan knew, was to hit the trigger finger. That chance was slim. But it was better than no chance at all.

Changing his sight pattern, Bolan took careful aim on the terrorist's finger. Drawing in a quick breath, he let out half of it and steadied his aim. The front sight still bobbed slightly, maddeningly. Then the slim chance faded into nothingness.

The al Qaeda man's hand had moved a quarter of an inch

to the side. But it had chanced the angle of the gun dramatically. Even if Bolan's bullet flew true, it would drive the trigger back itself. The terrorist's gun would fire on its own and, for all practical purposes, the Executioner would have shot the girl himself.

Suddenly the girl screamed at the top of her lungs and bent forward in terror to sob into her hands.

The man behind her was visible, still on his feet but leaning forward. Bolan didn't wait for the situation to change again. He fired two semiauto 9 mm rounds into the man's chest, then added another insurance round to the dumbfounded face above it. The entire process had happened in a split second.

Without hesitation, the Executioner swung the Uzi left again, ready to take out the final al Qaeda man on the stage. But before he could pull the trigger again, he heard the pop of a low-caliber pistol round and saw a tiny red hole appear directly between the terrorist's eyes.

Bolan saw what Professor Williams had been digging for in his jeans. The former OSBI agent had taken a seat again, and was using the back of the seat in front of him for a pistol rest. Gripped in both hands was a North American Arms .22 Magnum Minimaster. The barrel stuck out from the tiny revolver like the beak of some ancient predatory bird.

As he began to turn away from the stage, Bolan saw the professor pull the single-action hammer back with his left thumb and add another round to the face of the man falling behind the girl. "Williams!" the Executioner shouted above the roar in his ears.

The professor turned his way.

"Onstage!" Bolan yelled. "Get the girls out of sight!"

Williams nodded and started to climb over the seats. Bolan turned just in time to pump three rounds into the English-speaking terrorist with the close-cropped hair. The man had been racing down the aisle but was stopped in his tracks, jumping and jerking in a macabre dance of death.

Lawford and Theodore had dropped to their knees in the aisle, and were both sending rounds out over the seats at the terrorists who'd been stationed within the hostages. Farther up the aisle, the other Team One volunteers were doing the same.

Although the return fire was heavy, all around the auditorium, al Qaeda men were hitting the floor and falling over the backs of the theater seats.

Most of the students had followed the Executioner's order—or their own common sense—and dropped the floor. But a few seemed to be in shock and sat impassively in their seats staring straight ahead like zombies.

"Get down!" Bolan shouted again. Only one of the students seemed to hear him and obey.

The Executioner dropped to one knee, aiming out over the seats and tapping a trio of rounds into another terrorist. From the corner of his eye, he saw another man suddenly spring up from hiding two rows behind Lawford.

In one hand he held a Makarov. In the other a Tokarev. With a wild scream of fury he jumped onto the back of the seat in front of him and dived toward the OSBI director.

Lawford held the trigger back on his AK-47 and pumped the last four rounds into the airborne terrorist. The man tumbled out of sight.

Bolan drilled a trio of rounds into another terrorist as he

heard the OSBI director curse to his side. In his peripheral vision, he saw Lawford squatting over the bodies of the terrorists who had guarded them, searching for extra magazines.

As the battle had raged on, Bolan saw that Williams had cleared the stage and joined the fight.

As Lawford continued to curse and dig through the corpses, Bolan looked up the aisle in time to see a highway patrolman go down. It looked as if a round had struck him in the shoulder. But he didn't get up again as the Executioner turned in the direction from which the shot had come.

An overweight young terrorist—heavy acne covering his face and neck—stood near the back row by the doors. He was turning his AK-47 toward the Executioner when Bolan pumped a 3-round burst of fire into the man. Then, his own weapon locked open, empty.

"Here!"

The voice had come from behind the Executioner, and as he turned he saw Williams draw another Minimaster from his belt and toss it through the air. Bolan caught the flipping revolver with his left hand, transferred it to his right and thumbed the hammer. He was just in time to put the first round into the face of an al Qaeda man charging down the row of seats directly in front of him. The bullet caught the man in the jugular and blood shot to the side, raining over students who were crying, shouting and screaming.

An AK-47 fell from the man's hands, and Bolan grabbed it. Jamming the Minimaster into his back pocket, the Executioner lifted the assault rifle, dropped the magazine long enough to see there were still rounds in the box, then turned it toward the other side of the theater.

The battle was raging.

"Dammit Lawford!" Williams shouted behind the Executioner. "You couldn't find your ass with both hands!"

Bolan turned back in time to see Williams producing yet another revolver. The miniature weapon sailed through the air toward Lawford's outstretched hand. The OSBI man caught the gun much like Bolan had.

The members of Team One on the other side of the auditorium continued to fire. But they were not faring as well as the men on Bolan's side. As the fight continued, the Executioner saw that two of the men who'd come in as CNN cameramen were down.

Bolan started to weave his way through the seats, but the students on the floor prevented much forward progress. Jumping up on the back of an aisle seat, he raced across the chair backs like a speed-driven tightrope walker. Several rounds whizzed past him as he ran.

At the end of the same row of seats, he saw a gunman taking aim. Using his left hand for balance, Bolan fired the AK-47 with his right, stitching a path from the al Qaeda man's gut up to his chin. The man fell backward into the aisle.

Four members of Team One had gone down by the time Bolan reached the end of the seats and dropped down into the aisle. The pace of the battle was slowing. There was more time between bursts of fire, as more terrorists were taken out of the action.

Bolan saw a flash to his left, turned and saw the man who had been behind the podium suddenly rise from the orchestra pit. In his hand was an old Browning Hi-Power. He aimed it across the theater toward Lawford, Theodore and Williams.

He got off one wild round, and the slide locked back on an empty weapon. But the al Qaeda leader had already drawn the Katar with his other hand, and he turned toward Bolan and charged.

Bolan turned the man's head to pulp with a burst from the AK-47.

Suddenly, all firing stopped and the graveyard silence that had begun the fight signified its end.

The Executioner and the Team One members still on their feet—they were down to seven—hurried up and down the aisles checking bodies. As they did, the first members of Team Two came rushing through the doors. Several officers hurried toward the highway patrolman who'd been shot. They carried him out, and Bolan was happy to see that he'd been right about the shoulder shot. The man might spend a few nights in the hospital. But, eventually, he'd be going home rather than to cemetery.

That couldn't be said about the four men lying in the aisle where Bolan stood. There was no rush to get them out of there.

They had given their lives to save the students.

More of Team Two entered the theater and began herding out the students. They would be taken to one of the other buildings on campus, where each one would give a statement, then receive counseling. Bolan shook his head in amazement. Hundreds of rounds had been fired over their heads, yet there had been only minor injuries to any students.

As the auditorium cleared, Bolan made his way through the center seats to the right-hand aisle. He saw Lawford hugging a short, pretty girl in blue overalls and an orange T-shirt. Tears ran down both of their faces.

Theodore and Professor Williams stood next to the shattered CNN camera. On both faces the Executioner could see that odd mixture of emotion that always followed a successful battle. Victory, and the lack of casualties among the student hostages, had made the two warriors exuberant. But that exuberance was tempered by the knowledge that they had lost four of their comrades.

Bolan was about to join them when a Team Two man sprinted into the theater. "The bomb!" he shouted. "We've found it!"

BOLAN LOOKED ACROSS the parking lot at the rubble that had once been the Liberal Arts building. Was this the "big strike" al Qaeda had been leading up to? he wondered. Although the bomb squad had been unable to disarm the bomb, they had managed to evacuate the area in time. But even if all of the hostages had been killed, the body count wouldn't have come close to 9/11, and Brognola had indicated that whatever al Qaeda had planned was even *bigger.*

Bolan's phone vibrated. He flipped it open, pressed it against his ear and said, "Striker."

Ten seconds later, the Executioner no longer had any doubts that al Qaeda had an even more terrifying strike in the works. He knew what it was, and knew that tens of thousands of people were about to die if he didn't stop it.

What he didn't know was where it would take place.

16

Life, as he'd known it, had begun to turn upside down a moment after he'd stepped onto the elevator and pushed the button for the ground floor. As he'd turned to face the front of the car, Houston Burnsides had come sprinting out of his office at the end of the hall. The supervisor had yelled "Jennings!", and then the door had closed and the elevator began to descend.

Between the third floor, where Jennings's office was located, and the first, the Homeland Security man had done enough thinking for several lifetimes. He had realized that some type of silent alarm had been connected to his computer—an alarm that would notify his supervisor if he made hard copies of any of the nuclear power plant security evaluations. He felt himself flush with embarrassment as the light above his head told him he was passing the second floor. He should have known there would be such a safety device. There were a thousand and one different codes and passwords that prevented him from accessing the evaluations from his home computer. Why would he think something as low tech as printing copies and smuggling them out of the building would go overlooked?

The bottom line was he hadn't thought. He knew he had been so caught up in his international spy fantasy, and the hope that he would finally get in on some action that he had ignored the obvious.

The elevator came to a halt. Jennings realized that what was done was done, and there was no changing it. A sudden fatalistic resignation came over him. There was no turning back now—no story, no lie, no way to explain the fact that he had just printed copies of the nuclear power plant checklist, as well as the schematics and specific evaluation for the nuclear power plant in North Dakota, and had them folded in his jacket.

What Carl Jennings suddenly understood was that he had already lost his job. And if he didn't get out of the building before they caught him, he'd be facing a long prison term, too.

The elevator door opened and Jennings stepped into the lobby, forcing himself to act casual when what he really wanted to do was scream and bolt for the front doors. Across the room, behind a desk marked *Information*, he could see two uniformed security guards. One—an older man with graying hair and a big belly—stood gazing at a newspaper on the counter in front of him. The other, younger and slimmer, faced away from Jennings as he studied a bank of surveillance screens.

Jennings was halfway to the door when the phone on the counter next to the older guard rang. He quickened his pace as the man reached out with one wrinkled, lethargic hand to lift the receiver.

Jennings saw the guard's graying eyebrows arch in sudden surprise a second after he'd pressed the phone to his ear. He jerked, looking out across the lobby just as Jennings reached the door.

An alarm suddenly blasted from overhead speakers just as he stepped forward and pressed both hands against the steel bar on the door.

The door swung open onto the sidewalk, and Jennings saw the lock automatically shoot out to the side. He knew that every door in the building had automatically locked, and had he pushed on the door a second later, he'd have been trapped.

Adrenaline pumped through his veins as Jennings sprinted to the corner, turned left, then right at the next block. He ran through downtown Washington, with no real idea of where he was, or where he was going.

Finally, cutting into an alley, Jennings threw his back against the cold hard brick of a building and leaned forward, grasping his knees with his hands. His lungs burned as if he'd swallowed a blow torch, and every muscle in his body screamed in agony.

Where was he? What was he to do now?

What had he done?

Jennings reached into the breast pocket of his jacket and felt the folded copies of the checklist and North Dakota evaluation. Taking them to the Mossad man was his only hope for a future outside penitentiary walls. He would have to enlist the old man's help in getting out of the U.S.

A deep sadness hit Jennings. He knew he was about to become a man without a country. He had loved the United States of America for as long as he could remember. But like the mother willing to die for her child, or the husband who'd take a bullet for his wife, Jennings knew he had made the ultimate sacrifice.

He had traded his own freedom so that other Americans could have theirs.

Jennings walked casually down the street, getting his bearings. He had to think. He needed to contact Moshe Singer.

Jennings continued to walk, gradually feeling his pulse slow. He pondered his future. Once he was out of the U.S., what was he to do with the rest of his life? The answer came to him suddenly, and he couldn't believe he hadn't thought of it before. Israel would be grateful to him, even if the U.S. wasn't. They would also be impressed with what he'd pulled off, and he didn't see how they could keep from enlisting him in the Mossad.

Carl Jennings's heart was suddenly leaping again. He would finally get a chance to be the intelligence officer he had always wanted to be.

Spotting a phone booth farther down the block, Jennings hurried that way. Frank answered on the third ring. "Shamrock."

"Frank, It's Carl Jennings." He wondered if the slight tremble he still felt was audible in his voice. "I need to contact Moshe—you know, the old guy I've been hanging out with the last few nights?"

"Sure, I know Moshe," Frank said.

"Do you happen to have a number for him? Home? Or work?"

"Sorry," Frank said. "Don't have either."

Jennings cursed under his breath. He would have to wait. "No way at all to contact him before tonight then," he said as much to himself as to the bartender.

"I didn't say *that*," Frank said, laughing.

"Huh?" Jennings said.

"There's a way to contact him," the bartender said. "I could just hand him the phone. He's sitting right across from me. Came in early today."

Jennings felt as if his heart would jump right out of his mouth. "Put him on!" He realized he was shouting but at this point he didn't care.

A moment later, the familiar voice said, "Yes? Is this Carl?"

"It is," Jennings said, trying not to laugh out loud with delight. "Listen, we've got to talk. Got to meet."

"Meet me here," Singer said.

Jennings started to agree, then said, "No. They might know about the Shamrock."

"Who might know?" Singer asked. "Carl, what are you talking about?"

"Are you familiar with the Old Roosevelt Hotel?" Jennings asked.

"Of course. Carl, what is the matter? Are you in trouble?"

"I don't want to talk about it over the phone," Jennings said. "I'll explain it all when I see you." He paused, thinking. Should they just meet in the lobby? No. Someone might see the pages changing hands. It was better if they weren't seen together at all, by anyone. He would get a room. No, he'd have Singer get the room! Then, if the DHS was already on his trail, they wouldn't know the—

"Carl, are you still there?" Singer asked.

"I'm here," Jennings said. He felt good. He was thinking on his feet, proving he could carry out hairy, lightning-paced assignments. "How long will it take you to get there?"

"Fifteen, maybe twenty minutes with my bad leg. I could—"

"Go there and get a room," Jennings said. "I'll meet you there in half an hour."

Singer lowered his voice, and Jennings realized the man had finally caught on that something serious was happening. "I will register under the name Harold Goldberg," he whispered. "I will leave word that a Mr. Burstein is meeting me, and that they should ring me when you arrive."

THE LOBBY OF THE HOTEL was more reminiscent of a European country inn than a downtown Washington hotel. Cedar beams—once red, now weathered to a brownish gray—ran across the high ceiling. Mounted animal heads adorned the walls, and a huge collection of old music boxes was displayed on shelves behind glass along one wall.

"I'm here to see Mr. Goldberg," Jennings said to the desk clerk.

"Your name?" the desk clerk asked.

"Burstein," Jennings said. "James Burstein." As soon as the words had left his mouth, he realized two things. First, it had sounded an awful lot like Bond-James-Bond, which meant he just might be getting a little carried away and, second, Singer had not specified a first name for Mr. Burstein.

The clerk didn't seem to notice anything odd. He picked up the phone and tapped in a number. A moment later, he said, "Yes sir, thank you, sir," then looked back at Jennings. "Room 214, sir. Top of the stairs, to your right."

By the time he'd reached the second floor, Jennings was overflowing with enthusiasm again. He knew he might be regarded as a traitor by the others at Homeland Security. But in his heart, he knew he had done the right thing. And somewhere down the line, that fact might just come to light. Someday—a year from now, maybe ten—he might even return to the U.S. as a hero within the intelligence community.

Raising his fist, Jennings knocked lightly on the door. Singer, still wearing his camel-hair overcoat and snap-brim fedora, opened the door.

Room 214 was large, with a ceiling almost as high as the lobby. "Please," Singer said, indicating a rocking chair near the foot of the bed with a wave of his hand. "Be seated. And tell me what all this is about."

Jennings dropped into the chair and rocked back and forth a few times. Then he ground to a halt, unable to hide his enthusiasm any longer. "I've brought you something," he said, reaching into his jacket and pulling out the papers he'd printed in his office.

Singer smiled, and Jennings suddenly realized the man had to have known what he was doing ever since he'd called the Shamrock. Singer was an old hand at this game. They had talked about it the night before.

The Mossad man took the pages, shuffled through them and frowned. "This example," he said. "It is in North Dakota?"

Jennings nodded. "It was the only one I had time to get. But I can explain it to you if you need me to."

"You were hurried?" Singer looked up, frowning in concern.

Jennings nodded again. "I'm afraid I blew things," he said. "Some kind of alarm. I got away, but it means I'll need your help. I was hoping to go to Israel."

Singer had looked back down to the pages in his hand and

didn't answer. Before Jennings could speak again, he heard the sound of a door opening and looked up to see Frank, the Shamrock's bartender, come out of the bathroom drying his hands on a towel.

"Frank?" Jennings said. "What are you doing—?"

"I invited him," Singer said, still looking down at the papers. "Do not worry, my young friend. He is one of us."

Jennings was so taken aback he felt his mouth fall open. "Frank is?" he said. He shook his head in further amazement. He stared as Frank took a seat next to Singer on the end of the bed and looked down at the papers himself. "Are you Mossad too, Frank?" he asked. "CIA?" For all Jennings knew, the man might be from some other American intelligence agency who'd come to the same conclusion about helping the Israelis that he had.

Frank smiled. "We'll explain it all to you in a minute," he said. Turning to Singer, he said, "Everything there?"

Singer nodded, shuffled the papers and looked at Jennings. "So. What kind of help do you want from me?"

"Well," Jennings said hesitantly, realizing that what he had just provided the men might not actually be worth all he was about to ask of them. On the other hand, he had no choice— he had burned his bridges behind him. "I'm blown here. I've got to get out of the country. I was hoping Israel would be happy enough with me to offer me a Mossad position." He watched Singer hopefully. "After all, I *am* Jewish. Could you put in a good word for me, Moshe?"

Moshe Singer nodded his head but the smile had vanished from his face. "I could," he said, "but I don't think it would do you much good."

Jennings frowned at him, confused. "Why not?"

"You may be Jewish," Singer said, "but I'm not."

Jennings saw a flash. His hands flew instinctively to his throat. His neck felt as if it had been burned, and when he pulled his hands away again and looked down, he saw that his fingers were covered in blood. More blood was spilling out, and the men on the bed had risen and moved to avoid it.

Jennings was light-headed. He felt himself slide from the rocking chair as his eyesight grew dim.

"The men are ready?" he heard Singer say.

"They await our call," Frank replied.

"Praise Allah," Singer said.

They were the last words Carl Jennings ever heard.

17

"Quick!" Haji Farzanda, a.k.a. Frank the bartender, yelled. "Get the papers out of the way before they get blood on them!"

Kak Ishmail reached across the bed, grabbed the Homeland Security checklist and security evaluation, and jerked his hand away from the crimson spray issuing from the American's throat.

The men watched Carl Jennings die.

"Are they ready?" Ishmail asked.

"They await our call," Farzanda replied.

"Praise Allah." Ishmail looked at the body on the floor. Switching from English to Arabic, he said, "This man was a fool. But all Americans are fools."

"No," Farzanda answered. "We were lucky in finding this one. Not all Americans are fools, and you must never underestimate their capacity for cunning and deceit." He reached out, taking the papers from Ishmail's hand and looking down at them once more.

"I stand corrected," Ishmail said, bowing his head slightly. "But all Americans are *evil*."

Farzanda continued to study the top page of the papers in his hand. "With *that*, I will agree, my friend," he muttered.

But his mind was on other thoughts. Like, how best to accomplish what he knew he had to do next.

"Do you want me to make the call?" Ishmail asked.

Farzanda shook his head. "It is better if I do it." He looked up. "Your work is finished here," he said. "You have done well."

A frown creased Ishmail's already wrinkled forehead. "*Here*, yes," he agreed. "But now we go to North Dakota to serve Allah, no?"

"No." Farzanda shook his head. He walked to the bed, and lifted the *jambiya*. Slowly, he slid both sides of the Damascus blade across the bed spread, wiping off the American's blood. "There is no work for you in North Dakota," he said. "Your job is finished." He paused a moment, looking at the Damascus steel in his hand, inspecting it more closely to make sure no blood was still visible. "One nuclear explosion, however large, is still not enough to crush America. If we *all* died in it, who would be left to plan and carry out the next explosion? And the next? And the next?"

Ishmail stood frozen for a moment, then nodded. To Farzanda, it looked like his disappointment was tempered somewhat with relief. "Yes," he said. "I understand. You and I must live on. Even this nuclear disaster—even greater than our victories at the World Trade Center and Pentagon—cannot be the last. We must live to undertake even greater missions against the enemies of Allah." He paused for a moment, then said, "But eventually, I will be honored to die in His service?"

Farzanda almost shook his head at the man's naiveté. Ishmail was almost as big a fool as Jennings. For a moment, Farzanda wondered why he did not find the knowledge of what he was about to do unpleasant. After all, he and Ishmail had fought together since their days with the Taliban. "Oh yes," Farzanda said. "You will be allowed to die in Allah's service. In fact, sooner than you think." Without another word, he struck, slashing out with the *jambiya* and severing the jugular and all the other arteries, veins, tendons and ligaments in Kak Ishmail's neck.

"I am sorry, Kak," Farzanda said. "You have served me well over the years. And you played the part of Mossad agent better than anyone I have even seen. But you are old now, and more liability than asset." As the lifeblood pumping from Ishmail's throat slowed, he added, "You are linked to this stupid Jew on the floor next to you, and the entire American government will be looking for him. Should they have captured you in the process, I fear you would talk." He knelt next to the dying man. "And I have no intention of dying for Allah. Not now, not ever." Ishmail's eyes were fluttering, trying to close for good now. Farzanda reached down and held the lids open. "You may believe there is an Allah if you like," he said. "I recognize it as the children's fable that it is." He removed his hand from the other man's eyes. The eyelids fell shut, and the chest stopped heaving for air.

Haji Farzanda made a phone call.

"Abdul," he said. "Gather the men at once. The strike will be at the plant in North Dakota."

Haji Farzanda thought about both sides of this War on Terrorism. One side willingly giving their lives for a god that did not exist, the other stupidly believing they could stop men resigned to their own deaths.

It worked well for him. His bank accounts in Switzerland and the Cayman Islands grew almost daily, it seemed.

Farzanda quickly showered and dressed in a clean pair of slacks and shirt. He had a long flight ahead of him, he realized as he stepped out into the hall of the Old Roosevelt Hotel and closed the door behind him, turning the card on the doorknob to read *Do Not Disturb*. The men, all positioned on a remote farm in Kansas, had been centrally located until the exact strike site could be determined. Now, all that needed to be done was for him to study the security evaluation for the North Dakota plant, find the weaknesses and plan the strike. He could do that during the flight. His men would be there by the time he arrived. Then, as soon as the mission was under way, he would exit the area as quickly as he'd entered it.

He had no intention of being close enough to get hurt when the nuclear power plant went up.

The former Taliban fighter smiled to himself as he walked down the hall toward the old-fashioned staircase. Getting the security evaluation for *any* of the nuclear power plants in the United States would have been good, but this one—only a few miles from the northern U.S. border, was a bonus. The blast would affect a great deal of Canada, causing an international incident and a rift between two Western nations who traditionally stuck together in the face of terrorism.

Farzanda laughed out loud as he reached the bottom of the stairs, and walked across the ridiculously decorated lobby. If there was really an Allah, he thought, He would never have created men like him.

18

The Executioner pressed the cell phone tighter into his ear. "How long ago did this happen, Barb?" he asked.

"The alarm went off and the doors locked roughly thirty minutes ago," she said.

Bolan's jaw tightened. "Do they know who the Homeland Security man was who took them yet?" Around him, Lawford, Theodore and several other cops had stopped talking and were watching him. Across the parking lot, uniforms were beginning to inch their way toward the ruins of the Liberal Arts building as the dust settled.

"Yeah," Price said. "A guy named Carl Jennings. There was no prior indication he might be involved in anything like this. Lived modestly—well within his salary, and all that. Evidently he wasn't the most energetic employee they've ever had, and he was written up a few weeks ago for showing up with a hangover so bad he was worthless. But other than that there was no reason to suspect him."

Bolan held the phone to the side and spoke to Lawford. "Get me a ride back to the chopper at the football field, will you?" he said. "And advise my pilot to get the helicopter warmed up again." He turned back to the phone. "Do they know which power plants were compromised yet?"

"No," Price said. "Bear just caught the alarm on his computer scanner a few minutes ago, then tapped into the DHS lines to find out what was going on. My guess is he'll find the site before the Homeland people do themselves."

"My money's on him, too," Bolan said. A black-and-white patrol car pulled up. Bolan got in as Lawford circled the vehicle for the shotgun seat next to the driver, and Theodore got into the back on the other side. "I'm heading for the airport with Jack now," the Executioner told Price. "Call me again—as soon as you find out where we're headed."

The patrol car took off out of the parking lot, red lights and siren running code three. Bolan shook hands with Lawford and Theodore. "Goodbye, guys," he said. "And thanks."

"What do you mean, goodbye?" Lawford asked.

"We'll go with you," Theodore said. "This obviously isn't over."

"Sorry, gentlemen. I'm afraid I'm leaving your jurisdiction," Bolan said.

"So what?" Lawford said as the driver screeched around a corner. "We're assisting a federal agent, right?" He rubbed his chin, smiling. "If you've got jurisdiction, and we're with you, so do we."

Bolan looked at the two men. He didn't know exactly where he was going yet, but the chances were good he could use extra manpower. Phoenix Force and Able Team were still tied up, it would take several hours to get a team of blacksuits to him from Stony Man Farm, and he didn't like the idea of having to brief, then go into battle with, men he'd never even met before. "Okay," he finally said. "But I hope your life insurance is paid up."

"I'm worth a lot more dead than alive," Theodore told him.

The squad car stopped in the parking lot. The three men jumped out and raced through a gate to the football field, then across the turf to the waiting helicopter. They were about to take off when another OCPD car squealed to a halt next to the one they'd arrived in.

A man raced across the field toward them. The door was still open and he swung it back, then jumped aboard.

"Sorry I'm late," Professor Gary Williams said, grinning as Grimaldi took them up into the sky.

"That's okay," Lawford said. "You've never been anywhere on time in your life."

It took only a few minutes to return to Wiley Post airport. Grimaldi turned the plane's engine over and warmed it up while Bolan led the men into the rear cargo area. In the footlockers bolted to the floor, he found BDUs, boots and weapons for each man, then traded his own scorched clothing for a blacksuit. The Desert Eagle, Beretta 93-R, knife and the rest of his combat gear went around his waist and shoulders.

Grimaldi's voice came drifting back from the cockpit. "Ready when you are, Sarge."

The Executioner led the three men back to the passenger's area, took his seat next to the pilot and buckled himself in. They were halfway down the runway when his cell phone began to vibrate again. "Striker," he said.

"Even heard of Bathgate, North Dakota?" Barbara Price asked.

"Can't say that I have."

"Little village about fifty miles north of Grand Forks. Maybe twenty miles south of the Canadian border. Winnipeg is due north—another sixty miles or so."

"And that's where the nuclear plant's located?" Bolan asked as the jet's wheels left the runway.

"The plant's three miles southwest of town," Price came back. "On the Tongue River."

Grimaldi was staring at the Executioner. "Grand Forks, North Dakota," he said to the pilot.

"Is Bear sure that's where Al Qaeda's headed?" Bolan asked Price.

"Nobody's quite sure of anything at this point," Price said. "But Bear's scanned the DHS list three times now, and that's the only evaluation report that was printed out. The only other document printed was the security checklist itself."

"And nobody has any idea what's happened to Jennings?"

"Negative. He was out the door and faded into the woodwork by the time anyone realized what was happening."

Bolan remained silent for a few seconds, thinking.

"Barb," Bolan said, "if they've got the checklist and the specifics on this one site, it means they're going to study the report and look for the weaknesses that were found. They'll use the government's own study against them."

"That's my guess," the mission controller agreed. "They probably have their men in position, just waiting to find out which door to go in."

"They couldn't be in the exact position yet," Bolan said, "because they just identified their target." He felt his ears pop as Grimaldi climbed higher in the sky. "They know what they're going to do. But they just learned where they're going to do it."

"So they've had their people in a central location someplace," Price said.

"That's what I'd have done," Bolan said. "A central location like where I am right now. For all we know, they may have taken off in another plane from Oklahoma City at the same time Jack and I did. If not here, then it's someplace close."

"And it's just a short hop to North Dakota once you're airborne," Price said.

"It's a race against the clock at this point. Has anyone contacted the head of security at the plant yet?"

"No," Price said. "Hal just informed the President a few minutes ago. The Man told him to hold off contacting anyone, until you get there. He wants you in charge."

Below, the Executioner saw the flat plains of Oklahoma turn into the flat plains of Kansas. In his mind, he could picture what would happen once word of what was going down hit the federal law-enforcement community. There would be a turf war to end all turf wars, with every agency, administration, bureau and association trying to run the show. By the time they were through arguing the top half of the U.S. and part of Canada would be glowing with radiation.

"All right," he told Price. "Let's keep it all in the family, at least for now."

"Al Qaeda is bound to know we're on to them, Striker," Price said. "So they'll be racing the clock against us, too."

Bolan leaned back against his seat. "I need a copy of both the checklist and the Bathgate evaluation," he said.

"He's already working on it," Price said.

Bolan didn't bother saying goodbye. He just pressed the button, ended the call, then closed his eyes.

19

Only thirty people died immediately when the fireball blew the steel-and-concrete lid off reactor number 4 at Chernobyl. But high radiation within a twenty-mile radius resulted in 135,000 others having to be evacuated. Hundreds of other deaths followed, and during the next ten years the rate of thyroid cancer in children rose to ten times what it had been previously. The cost to the Soviet Union's economy had been over ten billion dollars, and adding that to an already shaky economy had played a large part in the collapse of the USSR a few years later.

Haji Farzanda knew Chernobyl had brought down one of the superpowers. But he did not kid himself—Bathgate, although it would be many times the size of Chernobyl, would not bring down the other. At least he hoped not. There was still money to be made, contracting to al Qaeda and other terrorist organizations. He did not want to kill the goose that laid the golden egg. There would be enough satisfaction in killing thousands of Westerners and contaminating an area of at least one hundred square miles.

You did not have to believe in Allah, Farzanda knew, to hate the West. There were a million and one other good reasons.

He looked out the window of the motel room. In would be light in another hour. He had slept during the flight to Fargo, but he was still tired. He was running on adrenaline, but that adrenaline would see him through the next few hours.

He would sleep as soon as he reached the Cayman Islands. Then he'd wake up and read about the terrible disaster that had struck the United States and Canada in a newspaper.

Farzanda turned away from the window toward the seven other men crowded into the tiny motel room. His eyes focused on the man at the end of the bed. He was the key to this operation. It would be won or lost with brainpower rather than manpower. As he continued to look at the man, he was suddenly struck by the contrast between him and the other six. He could not have found a man who looked less like the stereotypical Islamic terrorist if he'd tried.

Gregor Barakov had icy blue eyes, once sharp and alive but now looking slightly clouded. He had sandy blond hair, and his skin was light, even for a Russian. It freckled and burned easily when exposed to the desert sun. But Barakov's mother had been Albanian. The boy had been renamed Khalid Salih, and raised Muslim after his father's death during the early days of the Afghanistan occupation. That had not, however, prevented him from attending the university at Kiev where, under his Russian name, he had studied nuclear physics, and become Gregor Barakov, Ph.D.

Farzanda looked into the blue eyes now and saw the intelligence of a well-educated man overshadowed by the madness of a zealot. Barakov was every bit as crazy, and ready to die, as the other al Qaeda men. It would be his job to insure that all four of the nuclear reactors at Bathgate exploded.

Farzanda had to wonder how a man so smart in one area could be so stupid in another. Like the other men in the room, Barakov was looking forward to death.

Farzanda turned back to the window. He had studied the security assessment during the flight to North Dakota, and had found many gaping holes that could be exploited. The one he had chosen as the easiest, however, was the front gate in relationship to the plant's garbage disposal system. While nuclear waste was checked and double-checked, three large trucks came and went every morning to collect the regular, nontoxic trash. They were stopped only for a cursory search, then waved through. To add icing to the cake, the garbage company that contracted to the plant employed primarily illegal aliens. That meant a huge turnover in personnel, and new faces showing up in the trucks on a regular basis.

Turning back to the men, Farzanda said, "Our time is short. Even though the plan is very simple, we will go over it once again. Abdul, tell me what you will do as soon as we have hijacked the truck?"

The man leaning against the wall stood up and recited his responsibilities, beginning with the killing of the regular driver in the third trash truck, and ending with his final few moments before the nuclear blast. "I shall be singing praises to Allah when the explosion occurs," he said.

"And what do you do, Harun?" Farzanda demanded.

The man sitting on the floor recounted his duties much like Abdul had done.

One by one, the other al Qaeda men gave accounts of their specific tasks.

Finally, Farzanda came to Barakov. "And what do you do, Khalid Salih?" he asked.

Barakov looked slightly peeved to be going over it all again. But he was smart enough to know it was for the other men's benefit rather than his own. "I ride in the rear of the third truck—behind the scoop. I try not to be seen because I do not look like the others."

"But you *are* one of us—a child of Allah!" Harun said.

"If I am found, I remain calm and speak my English with the accent you taught me." He paused for a moment, then frowned. "Howdy y'all, my name's Joe, from Texas."

The other men laughed out loud at the strange accent. But Farzanda was satisfied with the words. They might not be perfect, but they would be spoken in North Dakota—a long ways from Texas. No one this far north would notice.

"Everyone's weapons are ready?" Farzanda asked.

Some of the men reached under the bed, some behind it. Two of them hurried to the closet, and one to the bathroom. When they returned, Farzanda saw their assortment of firearms. All had Tokarev pistols that had been captured from the Russians years ago, but kept well-maintained. There were three AK-47s with folding stocks. Two of the men would carry Uzis, and Abdul had chosen the one H&K MP-5 they had brought along. The only man without a long gun was Barakov. His job was not to shoot but to be protected until they could breach the security and enter the nuclear reactor area.

Farzanda nodded as he watched the men wrap their weapons and extra magazines in coats and blankets. They each wore one of the money belts he had provided to all of the men taking part in the American strikes. In each belt was a Kel-Tech

.32 automatic pistol. But unlike the men he had sent to Washington and Springfield, there was no money in these belts.

Dead men didn't need money.

Barakov spoke suddenly. "In which truck will you enter?" he asked Farzanda.

The question had come out of the cold, and the former Taliban soldier was slightly taken aback. Barakov looked surprised himself, as if the words had tumbled from his lips without his consent. Without missing a beat, Farzanda said, "I will be entering the power plant from another direction. I will proceed to the administrator's office in order to call the press and inform them of what is about to happen."

"How will you get in?" Abdul asked. "Without a garbage truck?"

"It is better that you do not know," Farzanda said. "If you do not know, you cannot reveal the plan should you be captured and tortured."

"Allah would never allow that to happen," Abdul said. "I would never—"

Farzanda knew the longer the discussion went on the more curious the others would become. Barakov had begun this line of questioning and, even now, the former Taliban could see in the man's eyes that the intelligence he had possessed before his al Qaeda indoctrination was resurfacing.

"Silence!" he said in a firm voice. "Allah has spoken!"

Abdul's lips slammed shut. The brainwashed glaze returned to the half-Russian's eyes, and Gregor Barakov became the unthinking, blindly following Khalid Salih once more.

Farzanda saw the first rays of light coming through the window. He rose to his feet, realizing he was witnessing what would be the last sunrise for the men in the room with him, and thousands of other people who were not yet awake. He planned to drive south to Fargo just as soon as the trucks turned into the plant. He had a ticket waiting for him at the airport, with connections that would land him on the island of Grand Cayman by nightfall.

But it was imperative that Barakov and the others think he was with them. So he held out his hands to the men, looked up at the ceiling, and said, "Allah go with us, my brothers. Today, we will awaken, together, in Paradise."

FARZANDA LED THE CARS off the highway and down a dirt road. A quarter mile later, he saw the lights around a small building. A dozen garbage trucks were parked outside the building. They would need only three.

The two-car caravan came to a halt in front of the building. As had been prearranged, Thabit drove his car to the other side and out of sight. Through a large picture window, the terrorists could see two tables crowded with men. Some had coffee cups in their hands, and cigarettes dangled from the corners of others. Many of them had looked up, peering through the glass, when the headlights of the vehicles had first appeared.

Abdul and Farzanda got out of the car with their weapons. Barakov had been ordered to stay inside during this portion of the mission. He was too valuable to risk losing to a stray bullet.

Farzanda fired first, and then suddenly he and Abdul were both drilling bullets through the windows and into the men around the tables. Glass shattered, and the garbage men jumped and jerked like puppets. On the other side of the room, the window on that side broke as Thabit and his crew started shooting. The table and floor ran red with blood, and then Farzanda yelled, "Cease fire and reload! Drivers! Go to your vehicles! The rest of you! Enter and finish!"

Abdul ran anxiously forward, stepped through the broken glass and into the building. On the other side, Thabit and one of his men entered. They circled the table, putting a final bullet into each driver's head. Barakov got out of the car and walked to the edge of the building and watched.

Fighting back the revulsion that threatened to break his resolve, Barakov walked to the trucks where the drivers waited. There would be two men to each vehicle, with him hiding in the rear of the third and final truck. He wondered again how Farzanda would enter the plant, but as he turned he saw the man sliding back behind the wheel of the car that had brought them. Farzanda would follow, he supposed, entering his own way when they reached the strike site.

Two minutes later, Barakov was hidden inside the garbage truck as it bumped up and down along the road. The loading mechanism consisted of a huge scooping device that threw trash deeper into the vehicle once it had been loaded, and it was behind this device that he hid. An inch of space separated the side of the scoop from the truck wall, and through it Barakov could see Farzanda trailing them.

The sun rose above the horizon as they drove down the highway. They came to a fork in the road, and Barakov felt his truck slowing. A moment later they stopped. He heard a door open and slam shut, then Thabit jogged to Farzanda's car.

"Which way?" he heard Thabit ask.

20

He hadn't known exactly how they'd come. There had been many security weaknesses sited in the DHS evaluation. And Bolan had spotted even more once he'd arrived at the nuclear power plant. But the ease with which he, Lawford, Theodore and Williams had rolled through the front gate—a simple flash of a badge had done it with no further ID required—had convinced the Executioner that the main entrance was a definite target. They had been dressed in battle gear, with M-16s and other weapons laying across their laps, and the gate guards hadn't batted an eye. So Bolan's first stop had been at the security command post located in the main office building. After reading the riot act to a cowering supervisor, Bolan had taken over plant security by sheer force of will.

Lawford and Williams manned the front gate in security uniforms. Bolan and Theodore had taken up positions just inside the main door of the reactor building. The rest of the personnel had been evacuated. Behind Bolan, only one door stood between al Qaeda and the nukes. A strong steel door that required a fingerprint and ID card to enter, but *one door* nonetheless. Bolan knew that was cutting it close. But he saw no other way to trap the men without alerting them ahead of time.

Tighter security at the front gate would mean waiting lines, and a waiting line would be as obvious as red lights and sirens. The al Qaeda operatives would have reconned the plant well in advance, and if they saw anything out of the ordinary they would simply back off and wait for another day. Time was always on the side of the terrorists, and they'd know that sooner or later, when nothing happened, things would relax again.

Unless the Executioner wanted to camp out in Bathgate, North Dakota, for the rest of his life, they had to get the men this day.

The line between Bolan's and Lawford's cell phones was kept open, and they had a three-way connection to Jack Grimaldi, who was circling the plant in the small jet. In his ear Bolan heard the OSBI director's voice. "Garbage trucks arriving," he said. "Guards say it's their regular time."

Two of the gate guards had stayed with Lawford and Williams to fill them in on the details they needed. "Tell them to do their usual check," the Executioner said. "No more, no less."

In the background, he could hear the heavy truck engines stopping at the guard shack. "Looks like Mexicans," Lawford said. "Probably illegals. These guys say that's not unusual, though."

"Pass it on," Bolan said.

"Jack," he added, "can you see them?"

"Just barely," Grimaldi said. "This thing ain't a chopper."

"Try to keep these trucks in sight," Bolan said. "See where they go. Garbage disposal was listed as one of the weak links in the DHS evaluation."

"I'll do my best," the Stony Man pilot said.

"Second truck's stopped now," Lawford said. "More Mexicans. More new faces. The guards say that's *still* not unusual."

Bolan gritted his teeth. He was surprised every nuclear plant in the country hadn't been blown up already if security was no better than this. "Okay," he said.

"Jack?"

"Still watching, Sarge. The first truck's turned a corner and pulled over. Looks like it's waiting for the others."

That didn't make sense to Bolan. Each truck would have its own route to save time. They didn't need to hold hands as they went around the plant picking up trash.

"Third truck," Lawford said into the phone. "Third set of new faces, all appearing to be Mexican."

Bolan was about to speak when he heard Gary Williams's voice in the background. *"Buenos días, mi amigos,"* the agent-turned-professor said. *"¿Como esta usted?"*

Barely audible above the sound of the truck engine, Bolan heard a voice say, "No hablo inglés."

"Well, *muy bien,* then, butthooks," Williams said. A second later he was on Lawford's phone. "It's them," he said.

"I heard," Bolan said. "Pass them through, then hop in the car and follow."

"That's a big 10-4," Williams said.

Grimaldi came back on the line a moment later. "I'm straight overhead," the pilot said. "All three trucks are in line and headed your way. But I'm about to fly out of visual again for a minute."

"No problem, Jack," Bolan said. "I think we all know what's happening now."

"Good," Grimaldi said. "There was a Chevy following the trucks before they turned in. I think they were together."

"What makes you think so?" Bolan asked.

"They stopped at that fork in the road you passed on the way in," Grimaldi said. "Lead truck driver went back and talked to the car."

"Go check him out, then," the Executioner said.

He turned to Theodore. The man held an M-16 A-2 at port arms and, even with his graying hair, looked very much at home in his BDUs. Bolan raised an eyebrow. "You've fired one of those before, huh?"

Theodore chuckled. "Once or twice," he said. "In the old days."

Outside the door, Bolan heard the roar of a large truck engine. "Let's see if you still remember how," he said. Throwing open the door, he stepped out onto the steps leading down to the yard in front of the building. All three trucks had stopped.

The Executioner aimed at the lead truck. The first round from his own M-16 shattered the windshield and drilled through the middle of the driver's forehead. The man riding shotgun had his door half-open when Bolan swung the rifle that way and switched the selector to 3-round-burst mode. His trio of .223s penetrated the thin steel of the door and he heard a scream. But return fire shattered the step below his feet, throwing chunks of concrete and white powder into the air.

Bolan dived headfirst down the steps, hit the grass on his shoulder and rolled to a kneeling position. From behind him, he heard the chatter of another M-16 and saw a tall, lanky, dark-skinned man firing an AK-47 fall to the ground next to the second truck.

Behind the garbage trucks, Williams and Lawford suddenly screeched to a halt. The two men dived out on each side of the vehicle. Williams had appropriated a Czech Skorpion from the armory aboard the Stony Man jet, and now a full-auto blast stitched across the back of another terrorist.

Bolan noticed that all of the men wore Western clothes and cowboy boots. Passing themselves off as Mexicans had definitely been their plan. Too bad they hadn't bothered to learn the difference between Spanish and English.

A tall, broad man in a red shirt with white pearl snaps suddenly whirled toward Lawford and Williams. Lawford had chosen a Mossberg shotgun. He pumped and fired, pumped and fired again. Both loads struck the red shirt squarely in the middle, and the al Qaeda man was lifted off his feet and slammed into the side of the truck he'd just exited.

Only two more of the terrorists remained, and both had ducked down under the middle truck. Bolan sent a spray of bullets skidding across the pavement under the vehicle and heard a howl. An arm flopped into view, and he put three rounds through the wrist. Another scream of agony met his ears, then the arm fell still.

On the other side of the truck, the final al Qaeda man panicked, crawled back out and lifted an MP-5 with shaking hands. Still kneeling, Bolan twisted slightly at the waist and sent another burst of fire into his chest. The man twirled like a top. As he came around past Lawford, the OSBI man pumped a 12-gauge round into his belly.

Suddenly, all was quiet.

Lawford and Williams walked forward.

"Check the bodies," Bolan said, glancing down. "And—" At the top of his field of vision, the Executioner saw movement. He looked up, and saw another man dressed in boots and western wear. But for a moment, he thought the man was one of the plant employees because he had blond hair, blue eyes and skin far lighter than the Executioner's own.

Then the man screamed, *"Allah akhbar!"* and raised a Tokarev pistol to fire.

Blasts from two M-16s, one Skorpion and a 12-gauge shotgun cut him down where he stood.

"Check the bodies," Bolan said when there were no more signs of life. They did, and a moment later the four men came together near the blond terrorist.

"Any idea who the hell Whitey was?" Lawford asked.

Bolan shook his head.

Theodore snorted. "Maybe another one of those American Taliban 'dudes?'"

"I don't know about you cops," Williams said. "But I know one English professor who could use a drink. Or two. Or twenty-five."

"We passed a tavern down the road on the way in," Lawford said.

"You silver-tongued devil," Theodore said. "You talked me into it."

Bolan nodded. The men had done their jobs, and done them well. Reaching into a pocket of his blacksuit, he pulled out some of the money he'd taken from an al Qaeda money belt...when? Yesterday? The day before? Last year? It seemed a long time since this mission had started with him viewing the al Qaeda training tape at Stony Man Farm.

Handing the money to Lawford, Bolan said, "This came from al Qaeda. Have a few on them."

DEATHLANDS®

Atlantis Reprise

GRIM UNITY

In the forested coastal region of the eastern seaboard, near the Pine Barrens of what was New Jersey, Ryan and his companions encounter a group of rebels. Having broken away from the strange, isolated community known as Atlantis, and led by the obscene and paranoid Odyssey, this small group desires to live in peace. But in a chill or be-chilled world, freedom can only be won by spilled blood. Ryan and company are willing to come to the aid of these freedom fighters, ready to wage a war against the twisted tyranny that permeates Deathlands.

In the Deathlands, even the fittest may not survive.

Available December 2005 at your favorite retailer.

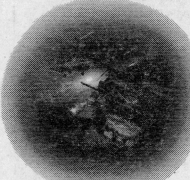